PENDRAGON

PENDRAGON

Mansel Jones

Goylake Publishing

Goylake Publishing, Iscoed, 16A Meadow Street, North Cornelly, Bridgend, Glamorgan. CF33 4LL
http://www.goylake-publishing.com

ISBN: 978-0-9566909-2-0

Printed and bound in Britain by Imprint Digital, Exeter EX5 5HY

To Daniela, Owain and Rhys

By the same author:

Fiction – Tangwstyl

Non-Fiction – A History of Kenfig

Chapter One

His name was Arthur. A man in his prime, he carried the title dux bellorum, the leader of battles. Charged by the Pendragon to defend the Britons, it was Arthur's task to hold back the Saxons as they sought to advance; it was his duty to ensure that the threat posed by the Saxon axes held fear no more.

Eleven times Arthur had raised his sword, Caledfwlch, against the Saxons, eleven times he and his war band had been victorious. To the Britons, a beleaguered and war-weary people, he was a hero, a man to admire and respect. To his war band, his teulu, he was a man to follow, a warrior of courage and wisdom. Yet to his mind, he was a failure, for his parents' murder had not been avenged.

Upon a fresh spring morning, Arthur was to be found striding across a courtyard towards a coastal villa. The villa was the birthplace of, and a home to, Ambrosius Aurelianus. Ambrosius was also known as Emrys Gwledig and, furthermore, he was the Pendragon and thus the leader of the Britons. Ambrosius' villa was not the grandest edifice ever built by the Romans, but it was one of the last to survive. Like its owner, it had weathered well; it had withstood the ravages of time.

At the main entrance, Arthur discovered two guards standing outside the door. Without hesitation, or the need for query, the guards opened the door, allowing Arthur entry. In his customary purposeful manner, the dux bellorum strode beyond the guards into the entrance hall. There, a basin was situated, strategically placed to collect rainwater from an opening in the roof above. To his left and to his right stood the guest rooms, devoid of any visitors, friends or family, for Ambrosius lived alone.

Experience told Arthur that Ambrosius would be found in the exedra, his place of contemplation. This room was located at the rear of the villa and to get there Arthur had to walk through the reception room into the inner courtyard. Columns surrounded this courtyard: four each to the front and to the rear, five each to the left and to the right. The columns, ornate, though lacking their original splendour, stood tall above the garden supporting a roof, a structure that protected the guest rooms and the perimeter of the garden path. The servants' entrance was situated to the right of this garden whilst to the left the guest rooms offered yet more accommodation.

After crossing the inner courtyard, Arthur reached the rear of the villa and the final range of rooms. These included a dining room, Ambrosius' private quarters and, central to both, the exedra, the Pendragon's inner sanctum. Here, Arthur knocked upon the door. He paused. Then, he responded to the word 'enter.'

The room was neat with everything in its place. The walls were painted a bright red while cream columns, complete with green leaves as a recurring motif, added an element of contrast. The dado consisted of dark red rectangles, dappled with ears of yellow barley, enclosing blocks of cream. The ceiling was red while the floor was covered with a mosaic. The mosaic was multi-coloured and it contained, within its central roundel, the head of Christ. The Chi-Rho monogram was placed behind Christ's head, forming a pattern depicting the sun's rays. The mosaic was the worse for wear, however, and some of the tesserae had been replaced. The repairs were largely slipshod with diverse colours and larger tesserae used to complete the pattern. Rugs, woven with a handmaiden's skill and an eye for detail, hid the worst of these flaws and, in addition, they provided an extra layer of comfort.

The furniture was sparse but serviceable. To the left a couch, complete with a woollen mattress and a leather cushion, sat against the wall while, opposite the doorway, a tripod table supported a tray and its contents. The items upon the table included a wine pitcher, two drinking vessels and an earthenware lamp. Furthermore, an iron footstool, crowned with leather, sat in front of a wicker chair. Arthur's gaze settled upon the man sitting in that chair; his eyes focused upon Ambrosius Aurelianus.

'Artorius,' Ambrosius said, preferring the epithet commonly used by learned men, those wise to the ways of Rome. 'As ever, I bid you welcome.' Glancing up, the Pendragon allowed his attention to wander from a roll of parchment held in his hands, to the tall, young man standing before him. 'You should take rooms here, at the villa,' he reasoned.

'I thank you for your offer,' Arthur said. 'But I prefer the familiarity of Badon and my roundhouse.'

After inclining his head in acceptance, Ambrosius rose from the wicker chair. Distinguished in the extreme, he had wavy grey hair, calm dark eyes, a firm chin and a noble Roman nose. His cheekbones were high while his cheeks were clean-shaven. The passing of the years had done little to diminish his military bearing; his strong, straight back, his proud, determined expression, his lean torso all spoke of self-discipline. His lips were generous though lately little moved to humour while his complexion, pure and unblemished, spoke of marble. To his enemies he was a man carved of stone; to his allies he was a rock, his country's foundation.

'An inventory.' Ambrosius thrust the parchment towards Arthur. 'It tells of every cow, of every horse, of every sheep held by the people of Badon. We need to extend this to the whole of Glywysing. We need to understand what the people can pay by way of tribute, what they can afford. We must ensure that we keep our soldiers well fed and well rewarded, but we must take care: we cannot afford to disaffect our own people, for we will need them; we will need them to take up arms when the Saxons advance. Do you understand?'

'I understand,' Arthur replied.

Ambrosius nodded, as if satisfied. He rolled up the parchment and placed it on the tripod table. Then, he reached for the wine pitcher and an earthenware cup.

'Now for more pressing matters,' he intoned while pouring out a measure of wine: 'What of the current Saxon threat?'

'Our borders are secure, but reports suggest that the Saxons are heading ever westward.'

'Then more battles will be fought.'

'If honour and our people are to be defended, they will,' Arthur agreed.

Ambrosius paused. Lost in thought, he poured wine into a second cup before handing that cup to Arthur. The dux bellorum waited while the Pendragon savoured his drink before doing likewise; the wine was sweet and playful on the tongue; it suggested to Arthur that there were advantages in keeping the trade routes open; there was something to be said for preserving close ties with Rome.

'I will be truthful with you.' Ambrosius stared into the depths of his drinking vessel, as though too ashamed to look Arthur in the eye. 'I am getting too old for such battles; I am growing weary of the fight.'

'Nonsense,' Arthur smiled. 'Without your leadership we would all be under the heel of the Saxons.'

'Without your strength and your sword,' Ambrosius challenged, 'I would have been replaced as Pendragon long before now.'

After placing his earthenware cup upon the tripod table, Ambrosius walked over to Arthur. Then resting his hands upon the dux bellorum's shoulders, this time he did look Arthur in the eye.

'You, Artorius, have been fighting the Saxons in my name for many years now.' While squeezing Arthur's shoulders, Ambrosius shook his head in resigned fashion. 'I am Pendragon, but in name only; my arm has grown weak, too weak to raise a sword.'

'Your arm is strong,' Arthur insisted.

'My arm is weak!' In annoyance and frustration, Ambrosius turned his back on Arthur. In anger, he clenched his fist and placed that fist against the wall. Then, after a pause and a deep sigh, Ambrosius unfurled his fingers, shrugged his shoulders and regained his composure. Becalmed, he turned to face his companion. 'I will not have flattery, Artorius. I know my strengths, and my weaknesses; I can no longer lead our people in battle. I am tired. I have given the matter much thought and I have decided to retire to the monastery at Mynydd-y-Gaer.'

Ambrosius had founded the monastery in his home territory of Glywysing and it was the custom for tribal leaders to retire to a life of religious observance and contemplation when entering the winter of their days. However, Arthur had not anticipated this path for the Pendragon; he saw Ambrosius as their eternal leader, if not in battle, then at least as their non-combatant commander.

Returning to the tripod table, Ambrosius selected another roll of parchment. After placing the parchment in Arthur's hands, he waited while the dux bellorum studied its detail.

'As you can see, I have called a Round Table. I have sent messengers throughout the land. I will nominate my successor when all the tribal leaders have gathered here in Glywysing.'

Rolling up the parchment, Arthur returned it to the Pendragon. Although his heart was heavy, he merely nodded, respecting Ambrosius' wish.

'Although I am reluctant to offer up agreement, I respect your decision. I wish you nothing but peace, should you retire to Mynydd-y-Gaer. However, I would remind you of one fact, namely that you have already nominated Pasgen as your successor.'

Ambrosius pursed his lips in thoughtful fashion. His gaze settled on the tessellated floor. Arthur had seen that look before. Doubtless Ambrosius was recalling the days of his youth, the days when the Romans had dominated the island of Britain. Some of the Britons had embraced Rome, had welcomed Rome's achievements and her rule, while others had harboured nothing but hate and resentment. However, as with all things, time must pass. Empires are made and fade, and so it was with Rome. Wars beyond Britain's shores called the Roman troops away and soon the islanders were left to defend themselves.

One man came to prominence, a man called Vortigern. The son of Gwidawl of Powys, Vortigern was also known as Gwrtheyrn Gwrtheneu or Repulsive Lips. Tall and thin, he was a strong, unscrupulous leader with little time for the ways of Rome. His ancestors originated from Ireland and, with their support, he became Pendragon. However, to reach such heights a man must encounter some opposition. And so it was with Vortigern. Although he carried many of the people with him, others rallied to Constantine's standard. Constantine had worn the purple; he had been a true son of Rome. More to the point, Constantine had fathered Ambrosius Aurelianus.

A decade of conflict led to the murder of Constantine, some say by Vortigern's hand. After this act, the boy Ambrosius was taken to safety; he was smuggled across the sea to Gaul.

Ambrosius was in Gaul and Vortigern was the Pendragon, the head dragon, the overlord of all the Britons. From that moment on, the island should have settled into a period of peace and tranquillity. However, men are not like that, and opposition remained. In fact, the opposition to Vortigern's rule intensified to the point where he thought it wise to acquire Saxon mercenaries.

For a decade or more, the Saxons fulfilled their role; they stood fearless as Vortigern's shield. Then, their ambition grew and they hatched a plan resulting in a slaughter, a slaughter known by the Britons as the night of the long knives.

In those days, it was considered impolite to carry your weapon into the feasting hall. Therefore, when the Saxons called a feast, ostensibly to discuss peace, the tribal kings, the most prominent men amongst the Britons, arrived unarmed. Needless to say, there was great slaughter, though Vortigern was spared. Forsaking his wife, Severa, he married a Saxon noblewoman, Rowena, and, for his trouble, the Saxons allowed him to keep his lands and the title Pendragon. However, from that moment on there was no doubt as to who was in control: the Saxons were no longer the shield; they were the sword.

Fearing for their lives, many of the Britons fled across the sea to Gaul. There, they joined forces with Ambrosius. Patiently, they bided their time until Ambrosius reached the age of maturity. Then, they followed him back to their homeland.

Vortigern was waiting, and the struggle was great, but Ambrosius would not be denied. He defeated the Pendragon and he restored lands to the descendants of the tribal kings.

By this time, the Saxons were strong and they held vast swathes of land to the east. From there, they launched raids against Ambrosius and the Britons. The need for unity was great, the need for peace amongst the Britons was paramount, and so Ambrosius was moved to make a gesture. Rather than fight the people of Powys, the people of Vortigern's homeland, Ambrosius agreed to allow Vortigern's son, Pasgen, to be their leader. In return, Pasgen and his people would support Ambrosius as Pendragon. Moreover, to seal the pact, it was further agreed that Pasgen would succeed Ambrosius as leader of the Britons.

With this act of statesmanship, Ambrosius secured the unity of the Britons. As one, they fought against the Saxons, sometimes pushing the invaders further to the east and sometimes forced into retreat, the battles raging for decade after decade after decade. For the Britons, unity had been achieved, but peace did not prevail as the Britons and the Saxons fought for their existence, as men of great resolve struggled for control.

'True,' Ambrosius reflected, his gaze wandering from the tesserae to the parchment, from the floor to the announcement that there would be a Round Table. 'I nominated Pasgen as my successor. Even so, I will not have that murderer as head dragon.'

Walking over to the couch, Ambrosius revealed a fine amphora, complete with two protruding handles and a narrow neck. The body of the amphora was plain, innocent. To the unsuspecting its contents offered nothing but pleasure.

Taking hold of the amphora, Ambrosius scoffed: 'A gift, from Pasgen. A fine wine, you might think, but no.' Sadly, he shook his head. 'The contents of this amphora leaked in the cellar and a number of rats took their fill. Of course, the poison killed them. Maybe we should take that as a lesson,' the Pendragon reasoned: 'be mindful of all creatures; they all have a place in this world.'

In sober tones, he continued: 'I am aware that my change of mind will cause problems. Nevertheless, Pasgen will not unite us and we need strength and unity to counter the Saxon threat. Time has moved on. Out of the need for peace, I nominated Pasgen as my successor, but he has grown impatient as the poison in this amphora demonstrates all too well.'

Abandoning the amphora, Ambrosius, once again, placed his hands upon Arthur's shoulders, facing him as a father might face a son, a son denied to Ambrosius the Pendragon. With a reassuring look in his eye and a fierce determination etched upon his face, Ambrosius said: 'Fear not, Artorius, for I have a good man in mind, a good man who will succeed me as Pendragon, a strong man, a man who will command the respect of all the tribal leaders. I feel sure that he will meet not only the challenge posed by my decision, but also the Saxon threat. In the meantime, I ask that you survey the coast, that you keep a keen eye out for the Saxons, for the menace of their keels; you will do that?'

'Of course,' Arthur replied.

'Then go.' Ambrosius thumped Arthur hard upon his shoulders. Then, he returned to his wicker chair. There he sat, his head back, his eyes closed, his lips moving in a whisper: 'And, if you find a quiet moment, take time to pray for an old man.'

Chapter Two

The following day Arthur and twelve of his teulu, his war band, were journeying east along a coastal trackway. They were on horseback, their preferred mode of travel. The cobblestone roads, built by the Romans, were largely overgrown and the Britons were wont to travel along ancient pathways and livestock trackways. Such a trackway ran along the coast, connecting Glywysing to Gwent in the east and Demetia in the west.

No Saxons had been sighted since Arthur's meeting with Ambrosius. Indeed, the only vessels to trouble the placid waters were those of traders, men from the distant east, merchants from lands often imagined by the Britons but rarely seen.

Arthur gazed out across the vast expanse of water, his eyes following the ships and their cargoes of wine and wool, of spices and oil, of jewels and honey. In the glory days of Rome, the coastline and the harbours would have been dense with such traders, but the Saxon wars had thinned their numbers until only the hardy and determined saw fit to trouble Britannia's shores.

Cai and Bedwyr rode at Arthur's side. Cai was also known as Cai Hir, Cai the tall. The son of Cynyr, he was a husband to Andrivete and a father to two sons, Garanwyn and Gronois, and Celemon, his beloved daughter. A warrior from the day he was born, Cai's face was distinguished by a mass of russet hair, one chestnut coloured eye and an eye socket disfigured by a scar. His chin and cheekbones were covered with a heavy beard while his skin was leathery, deeply tanned, apparently as thick as hide. Tall and broad-shouldered, he possessed large hands and arms that could lift a cart without strain. His legs were as sturdy as oak trees and, it was said, his feet threatened to create lakes when they trod upon wet ground. He wore a plain belted tunic, a long brown cloak and green breeches, made of linen. His boots were heavy and made of leather, laced at the front from instep to knee. A coat of mail protected his upper body while a sword hung from his belt. In addition, a close-fitting iron headpiece lined with leather was never far from his crown. Cai was from the uplands of Glywysing, a place renowned as a breeding ground for warriors. He carried the title magister militum, commander of Arthur's teulu.

In contrast, Bedwyr was a decade younger than Cai. The son of Pedrawd, he was the father of two young children, a son, Amren and a daughter, Eneuavc. From the lowlands of Glywysing, Bedwyr had studied at the greatest seat of learning known to the Britons, Illtud's monastery. Renowned for his prowess with the spear and the sword, Bedwyr was youthful in appearance with a thickly tousled head of fair hair and clear, blue, watchful eyes. The suggestion of a beard decorated his upper lip and his chin. From the lips of many women, it was said that he possessed handsome, calm features while his body was lean and lithe. That body was resplendent in a fine belted tunic, dyed and embroidered with many colours. In addition, he wore a red woollen cloak fastened at his right shoulder by a bronze brooch. Linen breeches together with leather boots warmed his legs. A leather belt encircled his waist, complete with an antler belt-buckle. A long iron sword hung from the belt, alongside a fine bone-handled dagger.

As Arthur eased his horse, Llamrei, along the trackway Cai was heard to mutter: 'I have been thinking.'

'Is that wise?' Bedwyr smiled.

'If Ambrosius is to nominate a new Pendragon,' Cai continued, his head held high, his ears ignoring Bedwyr's acerbic comment, 'then there can be but only one choice.'

'And who can that be?' Bedwyr asked.

'Arthur, of course. He is the only man who has fought for all the tribal leaders. He is the only one held in respect by all.'

'That may be so,' Bedwyr conceded, 'but Arthur is not a highborn noble; he cannot become Pendragon.'

'Yet, he was schooled in noble ways,' Cai argued. 'He is a man with a noble upbringing, a man with a noble background. More importantly, he is a man with a warrior's skill and the motivation to defeat the Saxons.'

Nodding, Bedwyr acknowledged Cai's truth, for, like Bedwyr, Arthur had also been educated at Illtud's monastery. True, Arthur's parents had been of humble origin but, through their labours, they had paved a way for their son. At Illtud's monastery, Arthur had studied the works of Homer and Virgil, Horace and Cicero. He had debated philosophy as espoused by Plato and Aristotle and gained knowledge of rhetoric, arithmetic and geometry. Furthermore, he had discussed the Word of God, the ways and the beliefs of the Christian world.

Arthur emerged from Illtud's monastery a Christian. However, those Christian beliefs were all but shattered when, in a brutal raid, the Saxons murdered his mother and his father.

'Besides,' Cai reasoned, pursuing his argument, 'Arthur has defeated the Saxons in more battles than I have fingers; the people will follow him; he is the only choice.'

'I thank you for your confidence, Cai,' Arthur said, while guiding Llamrei around a large and rather pungent cowpat, one of many that adorned the trackway, 'but it is our duty to support the man nominated by Ambrosius. After all, the main prize is not personal glory; the main prize is victory over the Saxons.'

With Arthur's words dominating their thoughts, Cai and Bedwyr and the rest of the teulu continued their patrol of the coastal trackway. Out at sea all remained calm. However, a little further into their journey the teulu was forced to halt as a number of men and horses were spied approaching from the east.

'Saxons?' Bedwyr asked, his neck craning, his muscles stretching as he endeavoured to obtain a better view.

'Fellow Britons,' Cai replied, his one eye, said to be sharper than a hawk's, peering into the distance. 'Their clothing suggests that I speak the truth. Besides, Saxons break out in a sweat if they try to ride on horseback.'

'If they are fellow Britons,' Arthur reasoned, 'then we have nothing to fear; let us ride to greet them.'

With Arthur in the lead, the men of Glywysing continued upon their journey until they came face-to-face with the men from the east.

'Who leads this party?' Arthur asked while raising his hand, indicating to his teulu that they should halt.

To his surprise, a woman emerged from the masculine throng, from a war band some one hundred strong.

'I do,' she replied.

'And you are?'

'Eleri of Ergyng. I am responding to Ambrosius' request for a Round Table.'

Ergyng was a territory to the north of Gwent. Therefore, Arthur reasoned, Eleri's people must have travelled south before continuing their journey along the coastal trackway. A province of modest size and power, Ergyng bordered the Saxon lands. The region was home to a fiercely proud and resolute people and, despite great suffering, those people had yielded no ground to the Saxons.

Upon Ambrosius' instruction, Arthur had spent many months in Ergyng organising the local defences. In those days, Eleri had been a mere youth, but now she had flowered into a beautiful woman, a woman beyond Arthur's recollection. Arguably, her most striking feature was her long auburn hair, hair that reached down to the small of her back. Her hair was matched by a glow upon her skin, a glow that suggested an inner radiance. She possessed dark, soul-searching eyes, smiling lips and a form that was both lean and sensual. She was blessed with elegant legs and dainty feet, although any hint of fragility was diminished by the look upon her face, a look of fierce determination.

In common with many women, Eleri wore a linen tunic, long-sleeved and diverse in colour. To facilitate horse riding, the tunic was short. Linen breeches covered her legs while around her shoulders there rested a mantle, secured by a brooch at her right shoulder. Her shoes were made of leather. Furthermore, a leather belt encircled her waist. From the belt, a small leather bag dangled playfully, together with a dagger. The daughter of Iaen, Eleri had no memory of her mother. One of five children, she was a sister to Teregad, Sulien, Bradwen and Cradawg, warriors all.

'I am Arthur,' the young warrior announced from his position astride Llamrei, 'dux bellorum to Ambrosius the Pendragon.'

'I know who you are,' Eleri smiled. 'Everyone knows of Arthur.'

'Where is your brother, Teregad?' Arthur said. 'It is my understanding that he leads the people of Ergyng.'

'Teregad was killed by the Saxons. They raided our border thirty moons ago. My brother met them with our teulu and he gave battle. We were victorious but, to my heart's regret, Teregad was killed.'

'For that,' Arthur bowed, 'I am sorry.'

'The Saxons have claimed all four of my brothers now.' In turn, Eleri bowed her head. She paused, to allow herself a moment of reflection. When she glanced up, however, a look of pride adorned her face; the look of confidence and determination had been restored. 'Even so, the people of Ergyng respect my family's nobility and they spoke with one voice when they nominated me as their leader.'

'Then I respect their wishes and I welcome you to Glywysing.' Arthur glanced over his shoulder, to the west, to the darkening clouds and the sinking sun. Soon it would be dusk and a place around the hearth would beckon. Presently Arthur would seek the sanctuary of his roundhouse and the comfort of his bed. He reasoned: 'I propose that we continue upon our journey, to ensure that we reach Ambrosius by nightfall.'

'Lead the way,' Eleri smiled. 'And be sure, I will be pleased to follow.'

Taking the lady at her word, Arthur led his teulu and the men of Ergyng back along the coastal trackway. The beauty of Glywysing lay before them, the gentle, undulating hills, the fertile fields, the rich green valleys ripe for pasture, the vast areas of woodland. Smoke could be seen in the distance, a faint wisp, as fumes escaped from a roundhouse and spiralled to meet the clouds. The smoke suggested a settlement and, soon, they would be upon that settlement and close to the villa and the hill fort of Badon. Arthur was about to announce that fact to Eleri when Cai demanded his attention.

'Boats!' the magister militum bellowed. 'Heading towards the coast.'

'Trading vessels?' Bedwyr asked; a hand placed to his forehead as he peered into the distance, shielding his eyes against the glare of the setting sun.

'Trading vessels they are not,' Cai judged. 'What we see before us are keels. What we see before us are Saxons.'

Chapter Three

Arthur led his teulu and the men of Ergyng away from the trackway, inland, to higher ground. Crouching, they settled on a mound surrounded by trees. Through the trees, they could see the sea and the Saxon keels. Those keels were getting ever closer, approaching the mouth of a river. In next to no time the Saxons would be upon them. In a little while, they would have to run or fight.

'How many men?' Arthur asked of Cai. 'And who is their leader?'

Regardless of his name, Arthur considered, he was a fearsome-looking man. He had a rugged face, dark, hooded eyes and dark hair. His hair fell lank on either side of his ears while a severe fringe exposed deep ridges upon his forehead. An iron-framed helmet covered with horn scales protected his head. His nose was notably large and a dark, drooping moustache graced his top lip. He had powerful arms and a solid torso, a torso blessed with an abundance of hair. Around his neck, he wore a pendant, an old Roman coin, which nestled amongst his chest hair. A fox-fur armband adorned his bare right arm while a leather belt encircled his waist. Upon the belt there sat a long, pointed dagger and an iron belt-buckle cast into the shape of a boar's head. He wore breeches of coarse linen, a sleeveless linen undershirt and a woollen cloak. The cloak had been worked in a variegated, closely set pattern of various hues and this item alone would have marked the man out from the crowd. However, to Arthur's eye, the cloak faded into insignificance when weighed against the large, sharp axe, an axe that rested comfortably in the palms of large, hirsute hands.

Arthur gazed at the man while Cai adjusted his position; standing, the warrior placed his shoulder against a tree. Peering beyond the leaves, Cai counted the keels. 'One, two, three, four, five,' he intoned, 'with forty men per keel.'

'Two hundred men,' Bedwyr reasoned. 'More than we have to hand.'

Arthur gazed through the trees, his stare settling on the keels. He noted the distinctive prows adorning the boats, the carved animal heads, fierce in their appearance. He viewed the Saxons, their helmets glinting in the fading sunlight. He judged that before a maid could milk a cow the Saxons would be upon the shore.

'What should we do?' Eleri asked, her face the image of concern.

'If the Saxons land,' Cai judged, 'they will cut off our path to Badon.'

'Then we have no choice,' Arthur decided, 'we must confront them in battle.'

Upon hearing those words, Cai smiled, his features displaying a grim satisfaction. Yet again, the moment had arrived, the moment when Cai would be tested; he would test himself against a fearsome opponent; he would prove to friend and foe alike that he was a warrior without peer.

After locating a secure channel, the Saxons navigated their keels beyond the mouth of the river. Rowing further upstream, they sought a sheltered place to land. As they disembarked, Arthur could see through their thick, matted beards to the features of each individual. Would Aelle be amongst them? Was he there, the man the Saxons acknowledged as Bretwalda, their Pendragon? Would he step ashore, the man who had slaughtered Arthur's parents?

'Who is their leader?' Arthur asked again. 'Aelle?'

Cai took a moment to pass judgement. While stroking his hirsute chin, he concluded: 'Their leader is Cerdic, ruler of Atrebatia.'

Once again, Arthur had been denied; he would not gain revenge for his parents upon this day. However, Cerdic was no mean prize. The ruler of a southern territory previously occupied by the Romans, Cerdic had made a pact with the Saxons.

He had formed an alliance with the invaders. He had traded with them. The people of Atrebatia had accepted Saxon ways and Saxon customs and had become familiar with the Saxon language. Cerdic had ruled his kingdom for sixteen years. A warrior of great experience, he had taken a Saxon wife. With his consent, the Saxons controlled the southern trade routes over land and by sea. With his consent, the Saxons were edging ever westwards.

'What are the Saxons doing this far west?' Arthur asked. 'Why have they deserted the safety of their home ground?'

'A raid?' Bedwyr surmised.

'This is a landing party, not a raid,' Cai suggested. 'Maybe they intend to meet up with warriors, further inland, or they are here to secure a foothold to allow others to land.'

The Saxons had secured their keels. Led by Cerdic, they occupied the far riverbank. The river was wide, but shallow in places while, further upstream, stepping-stones spanned the water, stretching from one bank to the other. Arthur decided that the Saxons would not reach those stepping-stones.

'Do you remember Tryfrwyd?' Arthur asked of Cai and Bedwyr.

Grinning, Cai nodded: 'It was a slaughter.'

'We will use the same strategy,' Arthur decided. Turning around to face his teulu, he met the eye of every man and he judged that his warriors were ready for battle. 'Cai, lead the teulu and half of Eleri's men. Ride out, confront the Saxons.'

Without hesitation or the need for further encouragement, Cai strode towards his horse, the men of Glywysing at his heel. However, at first, the men of Ergyng were reluctant to follow. Then, upon Eleri's instruction, a gentle inclination of her head, they too joined the teulu. With his helmet secure upon his head, Cai mounted his horse and with a bear's roar, he rode away from the shelter of the trees and the security of the mound.

'What about the rest of my men?' Eleri asked, her eyes wide, her pupils dilating. Arthur wondered if this reaction was due to fear, or the prospect of confrontation. Whatever the reason, he concluded, her eyes held a special appeal.

'The rest of your men are to remain here under Bedwyr's command; he will know the moment; he will give suitable instruction.'

'And what of my role in this matter?' Eleri asked.

'You, lady, are to remain here. If the battle goes against us, Bedwyr will lead you to safety; listen well, be wise to his words.'

After glancing at Bedwyr, and receiving a nod of acknowledgment, Arthur strode towards Llamrei. His heart rate had increased and his senses were sharp. His ears were alert to the softest of sounds, to an agitated dog, barking in a secluded settlement, to the somnolent waves as they rolled upon the shore. His eyes could detail the veins upon the leaves, droplets of evening dew upon the gently sloping ground, the various hues of the pebbles upon the distant riverbed. Despite the pounding of his heart and the surge of adrenalin heightening his senses, his mind was clear and focused. Once again, the moment had arrived. It was time to kill or be killed, time to defend the land, time to defend a way of life. It was time to raise Caledfwlch and strike a blow for freedom.

'Wait!' Eleri demanded. 'I will not have you nursemaid me; if need be, I can play a role in this battle.'

Arthur paused. Now was not the time for an argument. He turned to face Eleri. However, on this occasion, his thoughts were elsewhere; his primordial senses were captivated by images of conflict and combat, not by lust and beauty.

'I thank you for your concern regarding my safety,' Eleri continued, 'but I would remind you that I am a woman from a household of many men and that my father chose to be blind to my gender.

Be assured, I have bent a bow since the day I could walk and I can shoot an arrow as straight as any man.'

'Be wise to Bedwyr's instruction,' Arthur said, offering a dismissive reply. Then he mounted Llamrei and rode towards the river.

Arthur took his position on the crown of a knoll, looking down at the river. The Saxons were marching towards the stepping-stones, axes and spears at the ready, shields held close for protection. Soon, they would reach the stepping-stones; soon they would gain access to a nearby settlement.

On the far bank, Cerdic paused. Looking around, he stood tall, his features proud, determined. His gaze settled on the stepping-stones and he was about to issue the command to cross the river when the sound of a draco demanded his attention. The war trumpet split the air and Cai appeared to Arthur's left, charging, with the horsemen of the teulu in close attendance. They were accompanied by the men of Ergyng, some on horseback, some on foot, every man bellowing an oath or an insult. Words of profanity clouded the air, followed by a volley of spears, hurled by the Britons. United, the men of Glywysing and the men of Ergyng charged towards the river, only to encounter its natural barrier. Under Cerdic's instruction, the Saxons formed a shield wall, a solid mass of men, standing shoulder to shoulder. Not to be outdone they also hurled insults, expletives that provoked the Britons into an even louder retort. Despite the posturing and the threats posed by the spears it appeared as though the river would be the winner and that warrior would not confront warrior as man against man upon this day. However, with a wave of his arm, Cai instructed the teulu to ride downstream, towards the shoreline. Doubtless encouraged by their superior numbers, the Saxons broke rank; they ran along the far riverbank, shadowing their opponents. Nevertheless, horses can run faster than men and in their pursuit the well-organised shield wall was reduced to an irregular rabble. From his position upon the knoll, Arthur looked down with a sense of quiet satisfaction. His eyes sought the far riverbank and a line of trees and their alignment with the river. When the majority of the Saxons had reached that line of trees, he encouraged Llamrei and man and horse went charging towards the river. Unlike Cai and the teulu, Arthur could gallop ahead, for he had located the shallowest crossing point along the river. Surprising the Saxons, he rode through the cold water, swiftly followed by Cai and his warriors.

Immediately, Cerdic bellowed an order, a command to reassemble the shield wall. However, his men were too scattered, their numbers too thin to create an effective defence and so the teulu rode among the Saxons, slashing with their swords, stabbing with their spears, connecting with wood and flesh, leather and bone in equal measure.

Roars of aggression merged with howls of pain as iron cut through bone and sinew, removing limbs and scattering those body parts all over the riverbank. In one ferocious charge, Cai sliced through a Saxon's arm as the spearman thrust his weapon towards the onrushing mounted warrior. Cai removed the limb with one slash of his well-aimed sword and, as the wounded man fell to the ground, Cai spat Saxon blood from his lips, his secretion further staining the river.

In the last of the evening light slashing swords took on a bright blue hue as they struck Saxon axes, bending upon impact. Chalk and lime dust choked men's throats as that dust rose from the leather and lime-wood shields, forming a cloud over the battlefield, while horses rampaged over discarded animal-skin cloaks and spears of ash wood.

Despite their lesser numbers, the Britons held the advantage thanks to their horses and the scattered nature of the battlefield. True, the Saxons troubled the men of Ergyng, their axes and their spears forcing the warriors to the ground, wounding some, killing others.

After yet another charge through the scattered Saxons, Arthur pulled on Llamrei's reins, wheeling the horse around. There was just a moment to pause, to observe, as Cai, along with a number of the teulu, pursued a group of Saxons into the nearby woodland while in the opposite direction, heading for the coast, the remnants of Cerdic's men encountered a volley of arrows as Bedwyr and his archers emerged from their position upon the sheltered mound.

Nevertheless, through the carnage, Cerdic stood tall. Proud, defiant and surrounded by a determined band of warriors, it was clear that he was still eager for the fight.

Encouraging Llamrei once more, Arthur charged towards Cerdic's bodyguard, removing one man after another with little cost to himself until only Cerdic and his shield bearer remained. With Llamrei's white flanks dripping with Saxon blood, Arthur raised Caledfwlch on high before galloping towards the shield bearer. Armed with a spear, the shield bearer stood to Cerdic's left so that the axe man could hold his weapon in a left-handed grip and thus strike at Arthur's unguarded right side. Aware of the threat, Arthur took aim at the round shield and the painted image of a boar; with one well-timed blow, he shattered that shield, sending splinters of lime-wood into the air. The shield bearer was left with the shield's iron boss and its iron grip, covered in sweat-stained leather.

As Arthur charged once more, the shield bearer aimed his spear at Llamrei and he would have removed the horse's eye but for Arthur's swift intervention; in one dexterous movement the dux bellorum adjusted his grip, altered his hand position upon the hilt of Caledfwlch and thrust down, killing his adversary.

Llamrei's momentum took him away from Cerdic and, by the time Arthur had wheeled the horse around, the axe man had secured higher ground and was standing, axe held in both hands, awaiting his opponent.

Raising his sword, Arthur galloped towards Cerdic. However, before he could strike, he felt the bite of the axe as it grazed his kneecap. Although only a glancing blow, the axe had located an old wound and the ensuing pain made Arthur lose concentration. Before he could gather his senses, he was thrown from his horse. From his position, prone on the ground, he could sense Cerdic; he could taste the danger, akin to the tang of an iron bar placed upon his tongue, as the axe man bore down on him.

With an angry growl, Cerdic raised his axe. In a violent motion, he arced the weapon towards

Arthur's head. Blood from the axe rained down on Arthur's cheek, coalescing with mud and sweat.

Rolling to his left, Arthur felt the breeze generated by the axe as the weapon sank into the soft ground. Springing to his feet, Arthur scooped up Caledfwlch from that damp ground, tossing his sword from his left hand to his right.

On an equal footing, the two men faced each other, probing for a weakness, seeking an advantage. For both, the head and the advanced leg offered the best target. Carefully, slowly, deliberately they circled one another, each aware that a strike had to be accurate and effective, mindful that a warrior rarely received a second chance.

Physically, Arthur and Cerdic were well matched. In terms of their weapons, the Saxons preferred the axe to the sword. Wielded in two hands, the axe contained a blade wider than a man's hand span and a haft that offered a sweep greater than a man's height. In contrast, the sword was double-edged with a blade no wider than a man's wrist and a total length no greater than a man's leg and thigh. The blacksmith had crafted Caledfwlch to Arthur's personal specifications; a well-balanced weapon, the sword tapered to a point. Lighter than most swords, Caledfwlch's strength was its point and to be effective it relied upon speed and finesse as opposed to strength and momentum. Hacking blows from above the shoulder could leave the right-hand side of the body unprotected; therefore, Arthur preferred the straight thrust. With his eyes focused upon Cerdic's every movement, Arthur sought to make that thrust.

With a groan, Cerdic stepped forward, his axe swinging from left to right. Instinctively Arthur leaned back, removing his head from the flight of the axe. Encouraged, Cerdic rushed forward and Arthur felt compelled to retreat. However, the dux bellorum sensed that the axe man had succumbed to raw aggression and that he had lost sight of the boggy terrain and the nearby woodland.

Another grunt and another swing of the axe saw Arthur slip in the churned up mud. Cerdic also lost his footing thus allowing Arthur a rare thrust. The thrust drew blood with Caledfwlch grazing Cerdic's left arm. Enraged, the axe man swung wildly, his blows striking air, his aggression lost on the evening breeze.

In frustration, Cerdic raised his axe above his head. With all the strength he could muster, he brought the axe down in line with Arthur's left shoulder. The axe threatened to connect with flesh and cleave its way deep into Arthur's chest. However, wise to Cerdic's ploy, Arthur swayed out of danger and, instead of striking flesh and drawing blood, the axe struck timber and drew sapwood. With Cerdic temporarily disarmed Arthur seized the advantage; he altered his grip on his sword before driving the pommel up into Cerdic's face, dislodging two of his teeth. In a daze, the axe man tasted the bronze of Caledfwlch's pommel, as a second blow sent him to the ground.

With his sword poised, Arthur stood above Cerdic. To his right, he sensed that Cai was returning to the battlefield with the teulu for company but no Saxon prisoners. It was a harsh fact of battle that the chase brought out the beast in the man; many times Arthur had witnessed warriors, brave men, who had gathered their senses and seen fit to flee the battlefield, many times he had seen those warriors slaughtered by the chasing pack. To his left, he sensed that Bedwyr and his archers had been victorious; the rain of arrows no longer darkened the sky, instead those arrows lay embedded in mud or in Saxon flesh. Bedwyr and his warriors had crossed the river and now they were making prisoners of the Saxons, restraining the men who had discarded their weapons.

As the moon graced the sky and the ravens descended, Arthur stood above Cerdic, his boot upon the axe man's chest, the tip of his sword resting against the pulsing vein in the warrior's neck.

Through bruised and bloodied lips, Cerdic spat and mumbled: 'Finish me off; you know you will have to.'

'I will have to kill you,' Arthur agreed. 'But not upon this day.'

After dragging Cerdic to his feet, Arthur pushed him towards the approaching Bedwyr. Then, the dux bellorum glanced in the direction of the river. Sheathing his sword, he considered that it was time to wash the blood from his wounded body; it was time to cleanse his wounds and reflect upon the slaughter; it was time to make his peace and kneel before God.

Chapter Four

Standing before the river, Arthur unsheathed Caledfwlch and placed the tip of the blade into the ground. Then, kneeling before his sword, he thanked God for their victory. While in prayer, Arthur thought about his parents. Had he avenged their murder? How many Saxons would he have to kill before he found the answer to that question? Then again, would peace only come when he had defeated Aelle?

Rising from the sodden ground, Arthur wiped the mud from Caledfwlch. Carefully, he placed the blade into its wooden scabbard, his fingers caressing the outer coating of leather while the inner lining of oil-soaked wool embraced the weapon, ensuring that it would remain true in battle and stay free from rust.

As Arthur's body cooled and the adrenalin subsided, the pain in his knee became more intense. Sitting beside the riverbank, he removed a leather boot before rolling up the right leg of his leather breeches. Cupping water from the river, he splashed it over his wound, cleansing the gash made by Cerdic's axe. A stinging sensation enticed a grimace and that scowl remained frozen on his face as Eleri approached with purposeful tread.

'You are wounded,' Eleri observed, her slender frame casting a long shadow over Arthur as she stood before him. Her fingers tugged at her mantle, seeking its warmth, acknowledging the chill wind that accompanied the glimmer of moonlight.

'An old injury,' Arthur shrugged, making light of his abrasion.

'An injury made fresh by Cerdic's axe,' Eleri judged. 'Let me look,' she insisted, squatting with ease, running her fingers around the periphery of Arthur's wound, appraising the injury in delicate fashion. 'When we reach Ambrosius, you must apply a poultice of comfrey leaves and roots.'

'I will do that,' Arthur promised. After adjusting the leg of his breeches he stood, his tall, muscular frame relaxing, becoming languid, a look of ease playing around the stubble and the suggestion of a beard that adorned his face.

'Of course,' Eleri chided, her expression bordering on the coquettish, 'I should let you suffer.'

'For what reason?' Arthur frowned.

'For the harsh words you shared with me at the knoll.'

Perplexed, Arthur rubbed a hand over his stubble, his dark eyes betraying a hint of mischief, the smile on his lips revealing the true nature of the man. 'I berated you with harsh words?' he said.

'You refused my offer of help.'

'Ah,' Arthur mimicked the action of drawing back a bow, 'your skill with a weapon.'

'You refused me because I am a woman?'

'I have fought alongside women,' Arthur recalled, 'and I have seen those women display a ferocity greater than many men.'

'Then why not harness my ferocity?' Eleri demanded. 'You know that I fight for a purpose, that I fight with good reason.'

'You fight for your brothers.'

'I fight for my brothers,' Eleri agreed. 'And I fight for my land.'

The smile touching Arthur's eyes faded and his expression became sombre, thoughtful, as he recalled his own motivation, as he reflected upon his parents and their love of this land. Moreover, there is enough land for everyone, he considered, enough for everyone to live comfortably, in peace. However, some men would always want more; men, wealthy beyond all reasonable means, would always bully their neighbours, would always try to claim riches that did not belong to them. Such men brought misery to others; such men had no place in Arthur's land.

'Clearly, I was in error,' Arthur admitted, 'for you would have added strength to our teulu. I ask for your forgiveness and offer as my excuse a lapse into temporary blindness.'

'You lost your sight before the battle?' Eleri asked, a frown creasing her forehead. With her hand outstretched, she reached for Arthur, displaying her concern.

'My sight was all too clear,' Arthur confessed. 'If I was blinded, then I was blinded by your beauty.'

Eleri scoffed: 'Kind words, my lord Arthur. But I warn you, you will not win my loyalty through flattery.'

'Then how will I win your loyalty?'

'You will win my loyalty by regarding me as your equal; by respecting my status as head of my teulu.'

And with those words Eleri turned and walked along the riverbank, towards her war band.

As Arthur studied Eleri's proud walk, Cai approached from the battlefield. The warrior's skin and tunic displayed the blood of battle while fresh lesions added to the scars upon his face.

'How are the men?' Arthur asked.

'We lost four; the men of Ergyng lost many.'

Arthur's gaze wandered over the battlefield. Once again, good men had died, good men who should have been tilling the earth and tending their cattle.

'The fallen will return with us to Badon,' Arthur insisted. 'We will lay them to rest in home soil. I will visit their families and offer my condolences.'

'And what of the Saxons?' Cai asked.

'Gather up their weapons,' Arthur instructed. Inclining his head, he indicated a rise in the ground, an area of land that led to the woodland. 'Place their bodies over there. We will return at first light and bury the Saxons on the hillside, under those trees.'

Silently, Cai nodded; he would administer the task and call to mind a duty, a duty performed many times over.

Turning to Cai, Arthur said: 'We captured the living?'

'A battered score of Saxons.'

'Then they too will join us at Badon. We will hold them prisoner. They will labour in our fields and when the moment is ripe we will exchange them for our people.'

The sound of protest and Saxon expletives drew Arthur's attention to his right where the grumbling, shackled form of Cerdic approached, escorted by a smiling Bedwyr. As they made their way through the mud, Cerdic stumbled, only for the tip of Bedwyr's sword to bring him into line as it prodded the Saxon's broad back.

'What are we to do with him?' Bedwyr asked, his sword easing Cerdic to his knees.

'Shall I remove his head?' Cai grinned. With eager fingers twitching, his hand hovered over his sword, reaching for the hilt.

'Before you do that,' Arthur said, 'I would like to know his intentions; I would like to know why he brought his war band to Glywysing.'

The three men turned to face Cerdic. The Saxon, however, refused to look the Britons in the eye. Glancing to his right, Cerdic spat on the ground, releasing fragments of shattered teeth and fresh blood. Arthur observed that as well as the facial wound, a deep gash upon his left arm also troubled Cerdic, along with a diverse assortment of bruises. The pendant around Cerdic's neck, the old Roman coin, and the fox-fur armband reminded Arthur that Cerdic had reverted to the old religion. No longer a Christian, he followed the Saxons and their belief in Woden.

'He will not talk,' Cai reasoned. 'I suggest that we kill him now.'

'We will take him to Ambrosius,' Arthur said, calmly. 'The Pendragon will know what to do with such a beast.'

Cai grunted his reluctant agreement and Bedwyr was about to prod Cerdic to his feet when the Saxon glanced up at Arthur, the suggestion of a grin appearing upon his bloodied and bruised lips.

Climbing to his feet, the Saxon said: 'A Round Table has been called because Ambrosius no longer has the strength to be Pendragon.'

'And how do you know that?' Arthur enquired.

'This is the end for the Britons,' Cerdic continued, ignoring Arthur. Running his tongue over his battered lips, his assured expression suggested that he tasted victory and not the bitterness of defeat. 'Without Ambrosius the Britons will no longer unite.'

'I ask again,' Arthur said, his voice and expression calm, his countenance sublime, although he felt a quiet rage building, an anger developing inside. 'What are you doing here?'

Cerdic stared at Arthur, meeting him man-to-man, eye-to-eye, offering nothing more than a wolfish grin in reply.

Turning his back on Cerdic, Arthur marched towards Llamrei. After mounting his horse, he rode up to the Saxon, speaking with a calm authority in his voice and a cool look in his eye: 'We will take you to the villa. And, if you continue to play games with your tongue, then we will allow Cai to claim your head.'

Chapter Five

A new day dawned and Arthur observed as Cai and Bedwyr led the teulu back to the battlefield to perform the odious duty of burying the Saxon dead. Images of the battle had invaded Arthur's sleep. Nevertheless, he awoke refreshed, his subconscious mind exorcising the demons during the small hours of the night.

Throughout the glory days of Rome, people gathered and settled in towns protected by substantial stone walls. However, the towns were no more; they had succumbed to the burdens of taxation, administration and the Saxon invasion. Since the days of Arthur's parents, the Britons had retreated to the hill forts and reoccupied their ancestors' old home ground. The community had refortified the defences and the Britons had returned to a lifestyle familiar to their ancestors'; a lifestyle they had enjoyed before the arrival of the men from Rome.

Situated on a plateau along a mountainous range, the hill fort at Badon offered a commanding view of the terrain, which included forests, pastureland and arable land all sweeping down to Ambrosius' villa and the coast. Within its wattle and daub walls the hill fort housed a variety of wooden buildings including roundhouses, a chapel, a number of barns and kiln-houses for storing grain, stables and workshops. Arranged in an easy, random manner, as opposed to the rigid grid of the Roman towns, the roundhouses occupied the centre of the settlement, while the workshops and the barns adorned the perimeter.

A latticework of trackways had developed between the roundhouses. Arthur made his way along one of those trackways, passing hirsute men as they set about their daily tasks of tending their livestock, forging weapons and trinkets out of metal, repairing damaged structures and building new barns and roundhouses, anticipating that the coming season, the freshness of spring, would bring with it the beginnings of a good yield and increased fertility. Women, some pregnant, some carrying wickerwork baskets of farm produce, smiled as they encountered Arthur and he, being of generous and easy manner, smiled in return. Children accompanied their parents and assisted them with their tasks, while those too young to lend a hand ran among the open spaces, wooden swords or wooden dolls clutched in their tiny hands.

Upon reaching the stables, Arthur greeted Llamrei with a few soft words and a gentle caress as he ran his fingers through the horse's mane. From the stables, Arthur led Llamrei to the gatehouse, an imposing structure fashioned out of timber and stone. Strong, stone foundations supported the gatehouse, while two pairs of hinged double-doors, located at the front and rear of the structure, opened into the hill fort. Furthermore, archers atop a wooden platform also protected the gatehouse. The archers kept watch over the surrounding countryside paying particular attention to a cart-wide trackway that wound its way up the hillside.

Arthur led Llamrei through the gatehouse, pausing as a cart pulled by two oxen rumbled into Badon, its wheels creaking, its axles groaning, its owner sanguine as he chewed on a long blade of grass.

When free of the gatehouse Arthur mounted Llamrei, climbing upon the horse in one easy movement. His injured knee still troubled him, although the poultice of comfrey leaves and roots recommended by Eleri had brought some relief. Upon her arrival, Eleri had taken a room at Ambrosius' villa and it was Arthur's intention to greet her before noon.

The trackway was familiar to Llamrei and the horse could have negotiated his way down the hillside without guidance from Arthur. The main obstacles to negotiate were the defensive banks and ditches, the banks piled high with rubble and supported by wooden beams.

Once out into the countryside man and horse encountered more people from Badon working the fields. They were preparing for the feast day of St John the Baptist when they would light fires and lead their cattle out to pasture for the summer through the purifying smoke.

The sun was climbing high into a lightly clouded sky when Arthur arrived at the villa. Eleri's war band had made temporary shelters for themselves in the fields neighbouring the villa and, Arthur noted, they had been joined by the warriors from another teulu, the teulu led by Caradog Freichfras, who was also known as Caradog Strong-arm.

Arthur smiled as he caught sight of his old friend, Caradog, a man easily recognised in the midst of any throng. Short in stature with grey-flecked hair, which was thinning on the top, Caradog had a full beard, dark brown eyes and a battle-scarred face. That face often bore a pugnacious expression, an expression augmented by his barrel-chested frame. He wore a thick woollen cloak secured by a penannular brooch at his right shoulder, a knee-length woollen tunic and breeches of coarse linen. His boots were made of leather and a bone belt-buckle supported a leather belt, which encircled his ample waist. An iron sword hung from the leather belt and, as Caradog stood beside the villa gates, hands placed upon his midriff, thumbs resting easily inside his belt, Arthur reflected that he well-deserved the sobriquet 'strong-arm'.

From his position astride Llamrei, Arthur yelled: 'Caradog! You old fox!'

Glancing around, searching for the source of the commotion, Caradog creased his brow in puzzlement, only to relax his features upon catching sight of Arthur.

'So there you are, you young bear!' Caradog laughed. 'Get down from that horse and let me see if you measure up to my shoulder.'

The request was an old one, originating from the days when a youthful Arthur had fought alongside Caradog in his home territory of Gwent, a territory that bordered the Saxon lands. Even in those days, Arthur had stood far taller than Caradog's shoulder, but the old warrior insisted on playing his little game, his way of keeping Arthur, the young bear, in his place.

After dismounting and securing Llamrei, Arthur walked over to Caradog whereupon the two men embraced. Grasping Arthur's shoulders Caradog took a step back, to assess the young warrior. With a nod of approval and a glint in his eye, Caradog said: 'We will make a man of you yet. Although,' he added darkly, 'a man would be better served if he took a blade and not ribbons to his hair.'

'Jealousy will get you nowhere,' Arthur laughed, recalling that from the moment Caradog had set eyes on Arthur he had taken issue with the young warrior's long, flowing locks.

The two men paused as a cart rolled by, laden with a consignment of grain, grain that had been stored throughout the winter. A second cart contained fresh produce; fish, oysters, mussels, cockles and whelks, items for the feast to welcome the tribal leaders.

'You had a good journey?' Arthur asked.

Caradog paused before nodding, his attention taken by the cart and its contents of shellfish. 'Our path was free of Saxons. Although,' he added with a grin, 'I hear that recently you spent time blunting the Saxon axe.'

'We encountered Cerdic and his war band by the stepping-stones river,' Arthur confessed. 'We defeated the war band and Cerdic is now held secure in the villa.'

'What is Cerdic doing, this far west?'

'That,' Arthur admitted, 'I would like to know.'

'One war band in the heart of our territory would have little chance of success,' Caradog reasoned.

'My thoughts exactly.'

'Has Cerdic offered an explanation?'

'Apart from the occasional barbed comment, his tongue has remained silent.'

Caradog paused, his gaze lost between the villa and the distant, rolling hillside. After gathering his thoughts, he turned to Arthur and said: 'Maybe we should remove his tongue so that he remains silent forever.'

With that thought in mind, Arthur led Caradog through the villa gates and into the courtyard. Servants had taken the grain and the seafood from the carts and placed the items in one of the outbuildings - the kitchens - and now the empty carts rolled freely by, leaving nothing but a faint aroma to remind a hungry Caradog of their contents.

'How is Ambrosius?' Caradog asked, his gaze slowly wandering from the carts back to Arthur.

'He is strong in body and mind; he is in good spirits.'

'Ambrosius sent a communication stating that he is set on a future of contemplation, staring at the walls of Mynydd-y-Gaer monastery.'

Arthur nodded in agreement: 'That appears to be his wish.'

'His greatest wish is to see a return to Rome's glory days.'

'Maybe,' Arthur said, 'but those days have long gone.'

'Not for Ambrosius. Even so,' Caradog reasoned, 'you are right, Rome's glory days have gone and we must look to the future and secure prosperity for all our people. Ambrosius is the last of the Romans. All of which begs the question: who will bring prosperity, who will be Pendragon?'

'As you know, Pasgen was nominated, but Ambrosius thought it prudent to change his mind.'

'Very wise,' Caradog nodded sagely. 'The man is a barbarian. Although,' the strong man grinned, 'he will be annoyed.'

'Will Pasgen seek war?'

'He might ally with Vortipor, but if the other tribes oppose them, Pasgen and Vortipor will be defeated.'

Not for the first time, Arthur reflected that although Caradog could offer the appearance of an amiable bumpkin, he had a shrewd mind founded on solid commonsense. Caradog was right to suppose that Vortipor would ally with Pasgen because they were of common kin, tracing their roots to Ireland. Unlike Pasgen, Vortipor was a young man who had recently succeeded his father, thus claiming the leadership of Demetia, a large territory to the west of Glywysing. Arthur knew that Vortipor was an ambitious man with designs on the powerful region of Gwynedd, located to the north of Demetia. Arthur also assumed that Vortipor would lay claim to Powys after Pasgen's days, an act that would place him in a powerful position. Furthermore, a man who controlled Demetia and Powys could lay claim to the title 'Pendragon'. To Arthur's mind that thought was as unpalatable as the notion of the Saxons controlling Glywysing.

Turning to his friend, Arthur said: 'Maybe you, Caradog, should be Pendragon.'

The strong man laughed, a laugh that sent his shoulders into spasms of delight: 'Funny you should say that because when I've had my fill of ale I think the same thing!' Placing his hands on his hips, Caradog scowled at Arthur. 'No,' he said, shaking his head in decisive fashion, 'I am too old for the intrigues of tribal affairs; and besides, if Ambrosius nominated me as Pendragon that would mean war with Marc.'

Once again, Arthur concluded that Caradog was wise with his words. Marc held territory in Armorica and, more importantly, he was the leader of Dumnonia, a region across the sea and to the south of Glywysing. Dumnonia was a large kingdom rich in tin, a commodity prized by the Saxons, and the Romans before them. Strategically, the territory was important to the Britons because it acted as a buffer to the Saxons. Moreover, the vast sweep of its coastline ensured that the Saxons could not claim total mastery of the western trade routes and the western sea.

'What if Ambrosius nominates Marc as Pendragon?' Arthur suggested.

'That would mean war with Cadwallon and the men of Gwynedd.'

'Then,' Arthur concluded, 'there is no obvious candidate.'

'And yet,' Caradog mused, his short, thickset fingers caressing his hirsute chin, 'Ambrosius must have a candidate in mind.'

'We will have to trust Ambrosius' judgement.'

Slowly, thoughtfully, Caradog nodded: 'And trust that his judgement is sound. The man he nominates must keep us united as one. If not, the Saxons will claim the entire country, defeating each tribe, one-by-one.'

Chapter Six

Ambrosius Aurelianus resplendent in a sagus, a richly embroidered cloak, which he wore on top of a braided over shirt and a linen undershirt, sat at a round table in his dining room. Situated at the rear of the villa, the dining room adjoined the exedra, Ambrosius' inner sanctum. Rushlight candles and pinewood torches illuminated the room, flickering as an errant breeze wafted in through a crack in the masonry, dancing to the movements of the diners as they devoured their first course of snow-white bread and an assortment of shellfish.

At the round table, Arthur sat opposite Ambrosius, flanked by Bedwyr and Cai. Eleri and Caradog accompanied them along with two new guests, Cadwallon Lawhir and Archbishop Dyfrig. Cadwallon and Dyfrig had arrived at the villa separately, as the servants were preparing to light the candles in the closing moments before dusk.

Cadwallon Lawhir was also known as Cadwallon Longhand. The ruler of Gwynedd, he sat to Ambrosius' right, thus indicating that he was a guest of special status. In the prime of his life, Cadwallon stood a good head above his fellow Britons. He had a long, thin face, accentuated by a long goatee beard. His wavy hair touched his collar while his eyes were severe, hinting at an inner ruthlessness. His eyebrows were arched, his expression set, as though demanding the answer to a particularly difficult question. His nose was thin and, in keeping with the rest of the man, was elongated and pointed while his eyes and hair were brown, several shades darker than his weather-beaten skin. He wore a belted tunic, dyed and embroidered in many colours and a braided over shirt, glittering with gold thread. An antler buckle secured his leather belt and upon this belt sat his sword, a battle-weary weapon that had sliced its way through a fair share of bone and sinew, a weapon that had responded well to the care and refurbishment of the blacksmith's hammer.

Archbishop Dyfrig sat to Ambrosius' left. Known to many people as Dubricius, the man of God hailed from Ergyng. He had studied, and later taught, at the monastery of Inis Ebrdil. Dyfrig was a man of modest height, possessing a long, flowing beard that had turned grey many winters ago. His pate was bald; his nose was proud and noble, while permanent frown lines etched themselves into a strawberry birthmark, positioned upon his forehead. In addition, bushy eyebrows sprouted above eyes that were both watery and grey. Physically robust, save for a painful inflammation around his knuckles, Dyfrig carried no excess weight. He wore a long black cloak over a long black tunic, items that contrasted sharply with the colour of his beard and what remained of his hair. Invited to the villa by Ambrosius, it would be Dyfrig's task to offer God's blessing to the new Pendragon.

With shield bearers looking on, the servants entered the dining room, their arms weighed down with a selection of boiled and roasted meats, including beef, pork and mutton pieces, all flavoured with spices imported from Rome. In keeping with tradition, Cai was offered the choicest cut of pork, a thigh piece from the hindquarters, in recognition of his bravery upon the battlefield. There was a heavy silence and a long pause as Cai waited for someone to challenge him, to dispute his right to such an honour. Furtively, the tribal leaders glanced at each other, at the meat, then at Cai. When no challenge was forthcoming, Cai grinned; reaching for his knife, he stabbed at the meat, skewering a sizeable piece of pork before placing it to his lips. In approval, Ambrosius thumped the table with his fist, an action mimicked by all the tribal leaders, and, accompanied by a chorus of raucous cheers, eager knives carved the remainder of the meat while fervent fingers seized every morsel as the diners relished the moment of celebration offered by the feast.

'You present a fine table, in the best traditions of the Britons,' the archbishop said through a mouthful of spiced mutton.

'Maybe the Saxons would be more civilised if they learned the secrets of such hospitality,' Cadwallon reasoned, his knife carving a generous slice of pork.

'The Saxons will never be tamed,' Caradog grinned, revealing a fragment of beef trapped between his upper front teeth. 'For while we have a thirst for wine, they have a thirst for blood.'

'We cannot tame them, not with our swords. But God can tame them with Christ's Word,' Dyfrig said, his eyes wandering up to the ceiling, as if seeking the source of salvation.

'You propose to make them Christian?' Cadwallon asked.

Solemnly, the archbishop nodded: 'It is the only path to peace.'

'A fine aspiration to be sure,' Arthur said, 'but what of their belief in Woden? How do you intend to make the Saxons abandon that belief?'

'I will enlighten them as to the purity of Christ's message. Once they learn how to understand His Word, they will abandon their heathen ways.'

'I must say,' Cadwallon said, his tone bordering on the derisive, 'you have more faith in the Saxons than I will ever have.'

'I have more faith than you,' the archbishop said piously, 'be it in the Saxons, or be it in God.'

While reaching for an earthenware cup filled to the brim with wine Caradog grumbled: 'Such weighty matters are best discussed away from the feasting table, for heavy words do not aid the digestion.'

'Maybe such matters are best left to the new Pendragon,' Cadwallon suggested, his gaze settling on Ambrosius, 'for I understand that Pasgen is no longer in favour.'

'Pasgen disqualified himself by plotting against me,' Ambrosius said solemnly, his fingers tracing the contours of his own drinking vessel, his gaze lost in the depths of the wine. 'Pasgen tried to poison me. His actions have debarred all right to complaint.'

'So who will you nominate as Pendragon?' Cadwallon asked, his lean frame arching forward, the questioning stare, the look that was never far from his face now burdened with expectation.

'My choice will be revealed when Pasgen, Vortipor and Marc arrive. I understand that all but the latter have been spied on the road or sea; they should be with us tomorrow.'

Cadwallon sat back while nodding slowly, the suggestion of a smile playing around his thin lips, as though satisfied with the answer, as though contemplating wearing the mantle of Pendragon.

After the diners had consumed all the meat the servants stepped forward with fresh pitchers of wine and jugs of thickly brewed ale. The men at the table drank thirstily from their cups deliberately using their moustaches to drain the dregs of their wholesome ale.

The evening wore on, the ale continued to flow, then the guests called for a round of entertainment. A young woman stepped forward. Although she was slender of frame, when the first note escaped from her lips, it was clear that she possessed the voice of an angel. The young woman sang a song of unrequited love and the room fell silent. Enraptured by her voice the men forgot about their ale and, instead, they lost themselves in the melody and the melancholy of the song.

'A beautiful voice,' the archbishop observed when the last note had drifted into the evening air and silence had replaced the cries of adulation.

'A beautiful body,' Cadwallon said, his lustful gaze following the woman from the room, his shameless smile suggesting that he was contemplating an evening of delight: 'I would have her sing to me when I retire to my quarters.'

'I take it you've left your wife back in Gwynedd?' Caradog grinned, his fingers cleansing his beard and moustache removing the last of the crumbs and dregs of ale.

'A woman's place is not around the debating table,' Cadwallon stated imperiously. Leaning forward he allowed his persuasive stare to settle on the men gathered at the table until finally that stare alighted on Eleri. 'I offer no offence to you,' he added contritely, 'or to the people of Ergyng.'

'I take no offence,' Eleri said her gaze meeting Cadwallon's, her eyes unblinking. 'And as for my people, I will share your words with them, for they are pleased to be amused by fools.'

Eleri's words provoked a round of laughter, laughter that only subsided when the servants entered with the final course for the evening, a dish of fruit and pastries sweetened with honey.

After the guests had taken their fill of pastries, a group of musicians entered the room and began to play upon their instruments. A young man from Badon plucked and bowed his crwth, an instrument akin to a lyre, while a woman sweetened the air with her harp stringed with black horsehair. Furthermore, accompaniment was provided by a burly musician who blew upon a pibgorn, an instrument resembling a hornpipe complete with bells of cow horn to amplify the sound.

Then, a poet by the name of Taliesin stepped forward. Accompanied by the musicians he recited a tale of battle and honour, a poem dedicated to the exploits of Arthur:

'At Llongborth I saw slaughter,
Frightened men with bloody heads,
Before Geraint, his father's great son.

At Llongborth I saw spurs,
And men not afraid of spears,
And wine drunk from sparkling glass.

At Llongborth I saw armour,
Men, and blood being spilt,
And after the shouting a bitter burial.

At Llongborth I saw Arthur,
A brave man who struck with steel,
An emperor commanding the battle.

At Llongborth Geraint fell,
And brave men from the lowlands,
Yet before they were killed, they killed...'

When all the wine pitchers had been drained and the jugs of ale had been declared empty, the guests dragged themselves away from the feasting table and made for their beds. Aware that he had a wine-soaked head, Arthur decided to sleep at the villa. He was about to enter a room when Eleri approached him. With an outstretched hand and a look of expectation upon her face, she said: 'Arthur, I must talk with you.'

'And talk with him you shall,' Cadwallon said, his tall shadow appearing in the corridor, his angular features lit by a rushlight candle. 'But first I must have a word...'

Reluctantly Arthur nodded and he watched with a tinge of regret as Eleri made her proud way to her room.

'I hear that you defeated Cerdic and his war band at the stepping-stones river,' Cadwallon smiled, his bloodthirsty grin displaying his admiration.

Arthur nodded: 'I did, by the grace of God and the bravery of my men.'

'You lead a group of good men. However, I lead the most powerful territory in all of these islands; I have the right to become Pendragon, for I am the only man who can keep the Saxons at bay.'

'The first part of your assertion is true,' Arthur acknowledged, 'as for the rest…' he shrugged his broad shoulders, '...what are your words to me?'

'When I become Pendragon I will need to know if I have your support. I will uphold everything Ambrosius holds dear and I will uphold the common man's right to freedom and justice. Moreover, with your help I will ensure that all our people are protected from the ravages of fellow Britons and Saxons alike.'

'Noble words from a noble man.' Arthur took a moment to consider those words and their significance. Then, meeting Cadwallon's intense, ardent stare, he said: 'If Ambrosius nominates you as Pendragon you will have my sword.'

Cadwallon sighed, a deep contented sigh from a man who felt assured of his destiny. 'I knew that I could depend upon you. I look forward to hearing your declaration of support at the Round Table.'

Chapter Seven

Just before moonrise the following day, Arthur stood at the gates of Ambrosius' villa observing a war band led by Pasgen. The war band marched along a coastal trackway with eyes set on the villa. Pasgen sat astride an old warhorse, which plodded along steadily keeping pace with the war band. Even at a distance, Arthur could tell that Pasgen had aged since their previous meeting at Powys before the onset of winter. Handsome in his youth, Pasgen's face was now well lined and weather-beaten. His long, fair hair had given way to grey a colour matched by his generous goatee beard. His blue eyes were cool, still and clear. His sword arm, while not retaining its youthful vigour, nevertheless refused to wither with age. His hooked nose was slightly misshapen while his shield arm betrayed the scars of battle, revealing the occasions when his shield had failed. Pasgen wore a striped knee-length tunic, linen breeches and a long, flowing cloak. His belt supported a fine bone-handled dagger while his sword hung at his left-hand side, its weight taken by a leather shoulder strap slung over his right shoulder. His shoes were made of leather and tied with leather laces; furthermore, an intricate pattern of curves and knots decorated his leather scabbard.

Despite his advancing years, there was a belief throughout the land that Pasgen was still capable of creating a storm. Moreover, there was a general belief that a man could create the worst of storms when entering the winter of his days.

'Arthur.' Pasgen inclined his head acknowledging the dux bellorum. 'I note that Ambrosius has not deigned to greet me.'

'You will find the Pendragon in the villa,' Arthur said. 'I am sure he will offer you greeting there.'

With a shrug of his shoulders, Pasgen dismounted and Arthur turned his attention to a covered wagon and its occupant. The wagon contained a young woman by the name of Morganna, also known as Gwenhwyfach. Morganna had long, dark, flowing hair parted in the centre, dark, seductive eyes and lips that were both generous and sensual. Her nose was finely tapered with the slight suggestion of a kink at the bottom, a kink that was accentuated when she offered up a mischievous smile. Slightly shorter than most of her sex, Morganna had firm breasts, a slender waist and hips that were made for childbearing. Her limbs were too short to be graceful, her jawline too firm to be considered classically beautiful; nevertheless, she had about her an air of earthy beauty. That beauty was emphasised by the judicious use of berry juice to colour her eyebrows and ruan to redden her cheeks. Morganna was Pasgen's wife, the third he had taken during his lifetime, and she wore garments befitting her status including a purple cloak that fell to her ankles, a tight-sleeved under tunic that embraced her arms down to her wrists and a linen gown, which covered her upper body. The gown had wide sleeves reaching to her elbows, a body that sat comfortably upon her hips and a rounded neckline, which scribed an arc over the valley of her breasts. Between her breasts, she wore a necklace of amber beads, a wedding gift from Pasgen.

Morganna had a sister who was known as Gwenhwyfar. Considered by many to be the fairest woman in the land, Gwenhwyfar had been Arthur's lover. However, seeking wealth and a position of status Gwenhwyfar had taken to a nobleman's bed and word had reached Arthur that presently she was living the life of a highborn lady in her homeland of Powys.

As Arthur strode towards Morganna, a servant placed a short ladder by the side of the wagon and, after lifting up her cloak, Morganna made a regal descent. She paused in front of Arthur, a coquettish smile illuminating her face, a look of longing brightening her eyes.

Morganna said: 'You will accompany me to my room?'

'I will wait here,' Arthur replied, 'until the moon is high in the sky or until I have had the pleasure of greeting Marc.'

'You are a fool,' Morganna laughed. 'You place war before love; you place the suffering of the sword before the pleasures I have to offer.'

The seductive smile remained fixed on her face as Morganna made her sensual way towards the villa and her husband.

Later, the chill of the evening and the brightness of the moon told Arthur that he would not be greeting Marc that night. Furthermore, the same held true come the dawn when Arthur found himself in a room at the front of the villa sitting upon a bench beside a large oak table. Marc had not arrived with the dawn. However, the first rays of sunlight had brought with them Vortipor, ruler of Demetia. Vortipor was also known as Gwrthefyr. Of Irish ancestry, Vortipor had recently succeeded his father, Agricola, a man well liked and trusted by Arthur. Border clashes with Cadwallon suggested to Arthur that Vortipor carried with him the impetuosity of youth and that he was keen to make a mark and establish himself as a tribal leader.

Short in stature, Vortipor had a bald, shaven head, a bristling red beard and impish green eyes,

eyes that were given to settle on the ladies. His face was somewhat corpulent while his burly frame had been toned through hours of battle practice, although that frame had yet to be hardened through the exertions of countless battles. He wore a fine knee-length tunic, a leather cuirass complete with a metal-studded fringe and a woollen cloak that had been worked in a variegated closely set pattern of diverse hues. His legs were covered in bracae of brown leather, a hide that also warmed his feet. A leather belt adorned his midriff upon which there rested a dagger, but no sword, for that weapon was strapped to his back.

One-by-one, the tribal leaders took their place at the round table with Vortipor joining Pasgen, Eleri, Cadwallon, Caradog, Ambrosius, Archbishop Dyfrig and Arthur.

After glancing at each person in turn, Ambrosius brought the meeting to order with one heavy thump upon the table with his fist. 'Welcome, welcome, one and all,' he said, adopting his finest stentorian tones. 'Marc of Dumnonia is yet to join us, but we can delay no longer; we will commence the Round Table.'

A general murmur of approval was followed by silence as Ambrosius raised his hands, seeking order. When order had been restored and Ambrosius had regained the full attention of those seated at the round table, he continued: 'However, before we commence I ask Archbishop Dyfrig to lead us in prayer.'

Adopting the Roman attitude of prayer the archbishop sat with his hands outstretched. He took a moment to compose himself before turning his gaze up towards the ceiling. Then, as if in a trance, he said: 'Let each and every person here call upon God and request that He should bless us with His wisdom so that the deliberations of all noble leaders gathered at this Round Table can be just, unbiased and without prejudice. Moreover, we pray that our noble leader, Ambrosius, will enjoy long, fruitful days within the harmony of Mynydd-y-Gaer and its monastery. We also pray that the unity of the Britons will long continue and that our Saxon foes will see the error of their ways and thus commit themselves to the one true God. Amen.'

'Amen,' the assembly replied in solemn echo.

'And now my successor as Pendragon can be revealed,' Ambrosius intoned, his voice heavy, as though weighed down by the profundity of the moment. 'After much prayer and contemplation I have decided that Arthur should lead us as Pendragon.'

'This is an outrage!' Pasgen yelled. Placing his hands on the round table, he pushed himself to his feet. With his hands trembling, he leaned forward and bellowed: 'I will not accept this; I was nominated as Pendragon.'

'The noble lord is right,' Vortipor growled, his face a mask of vehemence. 'Ambrosius swore an oath, stating that Pasgen would succeed him and for that oath we pledged our loyalty to Ambrosius.'

'True,' Ambrosius said calmly. 'I swore an oath, and I swore that oath in good faith. However, that faith has been betrayed.' Turning to one of the servants positioned beside the wall, Ambrosius gestured towards a low tripod table. A wine pitcher and an earthenware cup sat upon the table, items the servant duly brought to the round table. Ambrosius watched as the servant transferred the wine from the pitcher to the earthenware cup. Then, while staring at Pasgen, the Pendragon said: 'I offer you wine, in good faith.'

'You have dulled my palate,' Pasgen said, while turning his head and resuming his seat. 'I have no desire for wine.'

'Let me persuade you,' Ambrosius demanded.

Abashed, Pasgen stared down at the tessellated floor. He paused, then he shook his head in decisive fashion. 'I cannot be persuaded.'

'I insist.'

'What game is this?' Looking up, Pasgen snarled, his bile rising to the surface, a layer of spittle forming on his lips.

'I suggest that you inform your countrymen as to the nature of your game.'

Pasgen's eyes settled on the earthenware cup and its contents of rich red wine. Meanwhile, all those gathered at the round table stared at Pasgen, their faces expectant, their expressions suggesting that they were eager for his reply.

'Very well,' Ambrosius said when no answer was forthcoming. 'I will explain. This wine is a gift from Pasgen. He will not drink the wine because it contains a poison.'

'The Pendragon lies!' Pasgen released his bile and with it his spittle, his discharge covering his section of the round table in indignant rage. 'I have no knowledge of the wine. If that cup contains poison then that poison found its way into the wine by another's hand.'

Unmoved, Ambrosius waved a lordly hand in the general direction of those gathered at the round table. With his granite jaw firmly set, he said: 'I trust to the good judgement of those seated at this table; it is for you, my peers, to determine who is telling the truth and who is telling a lie.'

'Ambrosius tells the truth,' Caradog said and, with the notable exception of Vortipor, there was a general murmur of agreement.

Smiling, Ambrosius nodded as if satisfied. He said: 'The contents of this cup and this pitcher make void the oath I swore at Powys. Consequently, Pasgen has disqualified all claims to the title of Pendragon. It is my judgement that he should hold on to his life and his lands and that he should be thankful that I show him mercy. I trust that all the noble lords here gathered agree?'

Again, with the exception of Vortipor, there was a murmur of consent.

'Then I reiterate,' Ambrosius said firmly, 'Arthur is my choice; he will become a noble Pendragon. Arthur is a true son of Rome and he will lead us well.'

'A true son of Rome?' Vortipor thumped the table in a show of frustration, his anger turning his face as red as his beard. 'If those words hold true then we are all condemned; Rome has failed us; Rome has sent no troops in years, not since the memory of our great-grandfathers. Indeed, Rome sends nothing but wine and God.'

'For once,' Caradog said calmly, 'your words hold true.' Turning to Ambrosius, he smiled: 'However, Rome does send a rather fine wine.'

'And the greatest gift from Rome is the Word of God,' Dyfrig insisted. 'We look to Rome for more than just military aid and fine wines and spices; we look to Rome for inspiration and for the nourishment of our souls.'

'Fine words, I am sure,' Cadwallon said, his displeasure evident in a frown that creased his forehead, 'but we overlook one salient point.'

'Then make your point,' Ambrosius said.

'Arthur is not born of a noble house. He has no right to become Pendragon.'

'Your words hold true,' Ambrosius agreed. 'Arthur was not born of a noble house. However, I nominate him for I believe that he is the only man who can maintain unity. He is the only man amongst us who can forge one voice from many disparate tongues.'

'Ambrosius is right,' Caradog stated firmly. 'Arthur has fought alongside each and every one of us. He has fought in every territory that we hold and he has led us to victory in many a battle. He is a man the Saxons fear. Also, he is a man our people respect. I would stand proud to swear allegiance to Arthur. Hail the new Pendragon! Arthur has my sword!'

Upon hearing Caradog's words Ambrosius nodded in silent satisfaction, Eleri smiled a warm smile of approval while Dyfrig glanced to the ceiling and uttered a quiet prayer. In contrast, Cadwallon looked on quizzically, Vortipor sat back and snarled while Pasgen shook his head in mock astonishment.

Sensing that his moment had arrived Arthur rose to his feet. Capturing everyone's attention, he addressed the assembly in a firm and steady voice: 'If I may be allowed to speak. I admit that I hold no ambition to become Pendragon, but I am honoured that Ambrosius thinks me fit for the task. Should our interests and petty squabbles distract us, I would remind you that the Saxons remain encamped at our door with a lust for further encroachment. With bravery and good judgement, we may yet hold them back. With unity as our main ally, we have a good chance of success. However, with discord, our borders will become porous and the Saxons will wash over us like a river in flood. In memory of our ancestors, for the security of our people and for the sake of those yet to come we must uphold our unity. Any other course of action would condemn us as traitors to this noble land. Personally, I want no more than that already held by my teulu and myself and thus I declare that the status quo should prevail. United we all have wealth, a measure of security, prosperity. As Pendragon, my aspirations would be to maintain that wealth, our security and our prosperity. With pride and humility, I accept Ambrosius' nomination. For the sake of our people, I request that all the noble lords here gathered around this table support me and thus bow to Ambrosius' wish.'

Climbing to his feet Caradog roared his approval. Leaning over the table, he glared at Pasgen transfixing him with a ferocious stare, a look normally reserved for the battlefield.

'Drag me to the gates of hell,' Pasgen yelled, 'and still I will not support you.' With his hands shaking through frustration Pasgen turned his back on the Round Table. With narrowing eyes highlighting a look of determination, he stormed out of the room.

'And what of you, Vortipor?' Caradog challenged, his glare settling on the ruler of Demetia.

'I stand beside my kinsman,' Vortipor avowed. 'I will inform my people that Pasgen is to lead us as Pendragon and that we have been betrayed by the so-called noble men of this Round Table.'

With his back as straight as his sword and with a look of daggers glinting in his eyes Vortipor followed Pasgen out of the room.

When silence finally descended, Arthur was moved to reflect that many battles were still to be won before he could stand tall as Pendragon.

Chapter Eight

Recently, mornings had not been a good time of day for Morganna. The sickness that accompanies the early stages of pregnancy had distressed her and she had resorted to the habit of reclining on her bed. However, on this day, the noise from the adjacent room and the Round Table gathering had disturbed her and she found herself with her ear to the wall, listening intently.

The argument had gone against her husband. Even though she had not been able to hear every word spoken, the tone of the voices told their own story: Pasgen would not lead the Britons as Pendragon.

That fact was confirmed to Morganna when Pasgen stormed into the room. For a moment, their eyes met and Morganna felt a frisson of fear as she glimpsed the anger etched upon her husband's ageing face. She concluded that she would be wise to leave him with his own thoughts and not engage in trivial conversation. Experience told Morganna that Pasgen would fight for his rights, that he would seek alliances, even with the Saxons, to achieve his ambitions.

Morganna turned her back on Pasgen and quietly she left the room. As she walked along the corridor, she reflected that she had married Pasgen because her father, Gogfran Gawr, had insisted on the union despite her protests and that she found Pasgen repugnant. However, she had to admit that Pasgen was pleased at the prospect of producing an heir. That thought enticed a secret smile, a smile that brightened her eyes; little did he know that the child is not his, she thought. Moreover, Morganna confessed to herself, little did she know who the child's real father was. In her hedonistic life, Morganna had enjoyed many lovers although she had to admit that none had brought real satisfaction and that was a shame because her desire had increased markedly since becoming pregnant.

Upon reaching the villa courtyard, the chill of the morning air compelled Morganna to adjust her purple cloak so that the garment sat snugly upon her shoulders. As she gazed at the hills of Badon, her thoughts lost amongst the trees and the greenery, she ran her fingers over her womb. She considered the baby that she was carrying and vowed that he, for the soothsayers insisted that the child would be a boy, would have the very best, just as she had strived for the best and that, one day, he would be Pendragon.

A babble of voices drew Morganna's attention to Arthur, who was talking with Bedwyr and Cai. As she admired Arthur's dark good looks and lithe body, she concluded that her sister, Gwenhwyfar, must have been touched by the moon to leave him for a nobleman of dubious reputation. Of course, Gwenhwyfar had left the nobleman's bed as well and she had found comfort in the arms of a man from the south; at least, that was Morganna's understanding of her sister's situation.

It was obvious to Morganna that Bedwyr and Cai were congratulating Arthur and she concluded that Ambrosius had nominated him as Pendragon. As usual, Ambrosius had made a good choice and although she could admit that fact to herself, loyalty to her husband demanded that she voiced her support for him.

A show of support for Pasgen would be nothing more than pretence, a casual deceit. The thought made Morganna smile because pretence and deceit were the bedrock of her marriage. Furthermore, she had developed a taste for treachery; in times of hurt and loneliness, she had discovered that duplicity and betrayal could be her friends.

Patiently, Morganna waited for Bedwyr and Cai to leave Arthur's side and engage in their daily duties. For a moment, Arthur was alone offering Morganna the opportunity to instigate her plan. In anticipation, Morganna moistened her lips. Then, she made her way across the courtyard to greet Arthur.

'Good day, noble warrior,' Morganna said while gazing up into Arthur's eyes.

In turn, Arthur inclined his head before offering an easy smile: 'Good day, noble lady.'

'I gather from your smile and from the sounds of congratulation that we are to acknowledge you as Pendragon.'

'Indeed, that is so,' Arthur said; 'it is Ambrosius' wish.'

'Such words will put Gwenhwyfar's nose out of joint when she hears them. She will want you back, back inside her house, back inside her bed. Do you want her back? Do you still desire her beauty?'

'Gwenhwyfar belongs to my past,' Arthur said firmly. 'She betrayed me. Nothing that she has to offer could encourage my desire.'

'And what of my beauty?' Morganna asked, her movements taking her closer to Arthur, her fingers reaching out as though drawn to Caledfwlch, as though seeking to caress Arthur's sword. 'Do you long for me? Could I encourage your desire?'

'You are a married woman; your words contain no substance.'

'Married and loyal,' Morganna lied. 'And, out of that loyalty I will offer you anything, anything you desire, if you will abandon all thoughts of becoming Pendragon and support my husband instead.'

While taking a step towards the main gate, Arthur shook his head: 'I cannot support someone who plots murder to achieve his aims.'

Throwing her head back in exaggerated fashion Morganna laughed long and loud: 'And what of you?' Briefly, she placed a hand to her mouth as if to control her laughter. 'Strike me if I utter an untruth, but many would say that you kill to achieve your aims. Is there any difference between the two of you? I think not.'

'I kill Saxons,' Arthur responded matter-of-factly. 'I kill them when defending this land and my people; Pasgen would kill a fellow Briton.'

'You are as swift with your tongue as you are with your sword,' Morganna said, making no attempt to hide the hint of admiration in her voice. 'No matter, my offer still stands. Support my husband and you can claim whatever you like.'

At the main gate, Arthur paused. He took a moment to gaze into Morganna's eyes and in that moment she willed him, beseeched him, to lose himself in their darkness, to submit to their seductive allure. However, instead, Arthur turned on his heel and walked out of the courtyard leaving Morganna to bite her lip in frustration.

Angrily Morganna turned and pranced towards the villa. She was about to enter the building when her attention was drawn to her bottom lip. Placing a hand to her mouth, she discovered that she had bitten through her lip and, in her frustration, she had drawn blood.

Chapter Nine

Leaving the villa behind Arthur walked east towards a small hill where servants from the villa were gathering dry brushwood. The servants placed the brushwood on top of the hillock in the knowledge that, should the Saxons attack, the kindling would be set alight and its flames would warn the neighbouring hill forts of the imminent danger.

Although Arthur's gaze was fixed on Beacon Hill, his mind was elsewhere, reflecting upon his encounter with Morganna. Without doubt, she was a sensual woman and in his youth Arthur would not have thought twice about her offer. However, the war with the Saxons had aged him and now he could honestly admit to himself that his priorities had changed and that her offer held no attraction. Furthermore, Arthur wondered at Morganna's loyalty to Pasgen. As with her sister, Gwenhwyfar, loyalty appeared to be a stranger, a shadow in the night, glimpsed and then gone.

Dark thoughts about Gwenhwyfar threatened to lower Arthur's mood, only for that mood to lift as he caught sight of Eleri. He observed as she made her easy way towards the hillock, her long auburn hair flowing in the breeze, her fingers absently trailing through the ferns in playful fashion.

At the base of the hillock, Eleri paused and smiled. With her right hand, she brushed her hair from her face before glancing up at Arthur. 'So,' she said, 'you are the chosen one.'

'In Ambrosius' eyes at least.'

'He is a wise man,' Eleri added her eyes narrowing as if to highlight her perception, a trait that was becoming familiar to Arthur, a characteristic that he was beginning to hold dear. 'Ambrosius is shrewd and prudent; he has made a good choice.'

'Does that mean that you and the people of Ergyng will support me?'

'I will support you,' Eleri said. 'And I will encourage my people to follow my lead. However,' she added impishly, 'there is one condition: you must do something for me.'

'If your request is within my power,' Arthur said, 'I will be happy to oblige.'

'Is prayer within your power?' Eleri asked in all solemnity.

'It is,' Arthur replied.

'Then come,' she said extending her right arm towards Arthur. 'Let us find a place of sanctuary and pray for your success.'

Together Arthur and Eleri walked east, following the twists and turns of the river as it flowed towards the coast and the villa, its water pure and clean. As they walked, they fell into easy conversation, although the subject of the Saxons and Arthur's role as Pendragon was never far from their thoughts.

'Some of the tribal leaders oppose your nomination,' Eleri observed. 'How will you persuade them? How will you secure their swords and their support?'

'By reiterating my words at the Round Table. By emphasising the need for unity against the Saxons.'

'And if you fail?'

'I cannot fail, for if I fail in my task then there will be civil war and that cannot be afforded because of our fight with the Saxons. It is bad enough Briton fighting Saxon, let alone Briton fighting Briton.'

Eleri nodded in solemn agreement. Then, in silence, they continued to walk until they were out of the ferns, their journey taking them to a trackway, a road established by the Romans. Along that road, the Roman soldiers marched further and further west, to the edge of the island they called Britannia.

Looking north, Arthur pointed towards the crest of a hill and a church that was partially hidden by trees. The walk to and from the church would take the best part of a day, a thought that pleased Arthur, for the best part of the day was when he was at Eleri's side.

'Up there,' Arthur said, 'a Christian church for the shepherds.'

'No,' Eleri said her voice firm and determined. 'Follow me, for I know of a special place where we can pray.'

Although Arthur's mind was troubled with questions, he chose to ignore them and, following Eleri's lead, he entered an area of dense woodland, rich with tall oak trees. The canopy of trees hid most of the sunlight and Arthur sensed that the air had taken on a chill, a sensation he experienced when entering a Christian church, a feeling that suggested to Arthur that he had stepped into a different world, the world of the ancestors.

After making his way through the trees, Arthur stepped down into a hollow. There he found Eleri kneeling beside a spring, a spring bubbling up through a fissure in the limestone. Eleri glanced up at Arthur and beckoned him towards the spring. As he stood over her, gazing into the water, she said:

'What do you see?'

Arthur bent a knee and stared more intently into the water. He had no idea what he was looking for; he had no notion of what he should say to please Eleri.

Gently, the wind rustled the leaves and the spell was broken. With a sigh, Arthur said: 'I see nothing but water.'

'Then we must pray to the spring god. We must pray that the god will grant you the vision to see so that you can glimpse the world of the ancestors.'

'By the laws of Rome and Ambrosius,' Arthur said, 'that is not allowed; we can pray only to the one true God, the God of Rome.'

'That is the law of Rome,' Eleri said, her gaze wandering from the spring to settle upon Arthur. Now she looked into his eyes with a measure of intensity, with the passion she had recently reserved for the spring. 'Even so,' she continued, 'many still pray to the ancestors.'

'To seek salvation we must pray to the God of Rome. Prayers to the druidic gods are forbidden.'

'That may be the law of Rome,' Eleri said, 'but even Rome cannot forbid something that touches your soul.'

With a look of serenity upon her face, Eleri turned to gaze into the spring. A shaft of light appeared through the trees illuminating the clear water. Reluctantly Arthur had to admit that the forest and the spring did offer a sense of serenity, a moment of peace far from the thunder of galloping horses, the lightning of clashing swords and the screams of injured men. The forest and the spring were a world away from the battlefield and yet in human form the gods of the trees and the springs had clashed with the God of Rome and such clashes had brought with them sacrifice and slaughter. Wherever you looked and turned, Arthur concluded, there was conflict and he wondered, had it always been so? More to the point, he considered, would it always be so?

'Will you join me in prayer?' Eleri said, her body arched forward, her face moist from droplets of spring water.

'I cannot pray to a spring god.'

'Then I will pray for unity amongst the Britons and I will pray for you. I will pray that you will have the good fortune to lead us as Pendragon and that you will find a path to peace.'

In silence, Arthur observed as Eleri made her peace with the spring god. He felt no animosity towards her, no hatred, no desire to drag her from this place. At the same time, he felt no urge to join her in prayer. However, as Eleri rose to her feet Arthur offered his hand and together they walked away from the spring.

'You are not a daughter of Rome,' Arthur said as they climbed out of the hollow.

'That is true,' Eleri smiled. 'I was brought up with the customs of Rome but, with each brother's passing, I searched for another way to ease my pain. A wise man enlightened me to the old, druidic beliefs and through those beliefs I found peace. I do not despise Dyfrig and his faith and I am happy to play a part in his rituals and ceremonies. Yet, for me, peace can only be found beside the springs and in the woodlands, those places deemed sacred by the druids. As Pendragon, will you allow any man or any woman to pray to the god of their choice?'

'I cannot allow such freedom.'

'Why do you utter such words?'

'Because the old beliefs stand for human sacrifice; Caesar said so.'

'They do not,' Eleri said vehemently. 'I have sacrificed no one and I have seen no one sacrificed. The druids' aim is to enrich life, to share knowledge, to enable everyone to find peace through the ancestors. I pray to the ancestors. My family, my brothers, have become gods and their souls have become immortal. I find peace through prayer, through praying to their souls. Believe me, Caesar and your Roman tutors have misled you.'

Arthur was about to challenge that point with a firm argument of his own when his attention was taken by a disturbance in the forest. The crack of dry brushwood and the waving of a branch told him that something other than a forest animal or the breeze was at play. Indeed, the disturbance told him that someone had followed their footsteps into the forest.

Drawing his sword, Arthur indicated to Eleri that she should maintain her position beside a large oak tree. Without argument or the thought of contradiction, she did so. With sword in hand, Arthur made his light-footed way to the source of the disturbance. Beside another oak tree and upon a branch, he found no one and no thing, except for a few strands from a garment, which confirmed his suspicions.

Arthur placed the strands in the palm of his left hand. The strands were multicoloured and they had been worked into a closely set pattern that suggested a garment of some quality and expense. Arthur decided to keep the strands for they might suggest who had seen fit to follow him into the forest.

Arthur was still gazing at the strands when he sensed Eleri at his side. While glancing at the strands she said: 'Who was there?'

'I do not know,' Arthur replied his mind considering the possibilities and resting upon the tribal leaders gathered at the Round Table. 'Come,' he said, 'the day moves on; we must return to the villa.'

At first Eleri held her ground, her face a mixture of uncertainty and concern. 'Will you betray me?' she asked.

'You know that I will not betray you. But we should leave this place and pray to God that no ill is born of this venture.'

Chapter Ten

The following day the tribal leaders once again gathered at the villa. With Ambrosius in command, they took their seats and awaited his instructions. Arthur allowed his eyes to wander around the table settling on Ambrosius, Archbishop Dyfrig, Caradog, Cadwallon, Vortipor and Eleri. The one notable absentee was Pasgen and Arthur could only wonder at the reason for his absence.

In customary fashion, Ambrosius glanced at each person in turn, then he brought the meeting to order, his fist applying one heavy thump upon the table. 'Welcome to our second Round Table,' he said in a firm, commanding voice. 'Before we commence, I will ask Archbishop Dyfrig to lead us in prayer.'

In response, Archbishop Dyfrig was about to raise his hands and stretch them across the table when Vortipor of Demetia leapt to his feet.

'Wait!' the leader of the Demetians said. 'We are forgetting one person; where is my kinsman, Pasgen?'

Cadwallon glanced at Caradog, Ambrosius glanced at Arthur and Dyfrig glanced at Eleri. However, no one could provide an answer.

'Pasgen will not arrive,' Vortipor continued, 'not even if we wait until the moon is fished from the sea.'

'Why will Pasgen not arrive?' Ambrosius asked. 'Has he returned to his homeland?'

'Yesterday,' Vortipor said, his rotund face and bald head glowing, matching the colour of his prickly, red beard as the heat in his body rose to complement the passion of the occasion, 'I followed Eleri of Ergyng and I saw her and Arthur visit a druidic shrine. They are both heretics. Arthur's claim to Pendragon is disqualified and Eleri should be punished because she made Pasgen disappear through druidic magic.'

An audible intake of breath from those seated at the Round Table was quickly followed by a babble of voices as the tribal leaders sought to make sense of Vortipor's announcement. Meanwhile, Arthur kept his silence, his gaze wandering from the fragments of thread held in his left hand to Vortipor's woollen cloak. In Arthur's mind there was no doubt: the diverse, closely set pattern upon the threads matched those of the cloak.

As the babble of voices threatened to build into a cacophony of sound Ambrosius thumped the table in an effort to restore order. 'Silence!' he demanded and an uneasy peace descended on the room. When order had been restored Ambrosius continued: 'Why would Eleri of Ergyng make Pasgen disappear?'

'That is obvious,' Vortipor replied, 'to remove opposition to Arthur, to clear his path to the title of Pendragon.'

'And yet I know Eleri to be loyal to our God,' Dyfrig said, the permanent frown lines upon his forehead becoming deeper, his grey, bushy eyebrows obscuring his watery eyes. Thoughtfully, the archbishop stroked his long, grey beard: 'My lord Vortipor, are you sure of your words?'

'I am sure,' Vortipor said confidently, the smile upon his face revealing a youthful arrogance, a measure of contentment, displaying the certainty of victory. 'I can lead you to the spring, if that is your wish. The ground has been disturbed. Your eyes will witness the truth.'

With spittle forming on his lips, Archbishop Dyfrig struggled to control his emotions. His hands, painfully inflamed around the knuckles, shook as he challenged Eleri: 'How can you acknowledge Rome and at the same time worship druidic gods?'

Calmly, Eleri rose to her feet. The determination in her eyes offered a challenge to the tribal leaders, a challenge Vortipor saw fit to avoid as he averted his gaze. 'What I do is not extraordinary,' she said. 'Indeed, my beliefs are echoed by many of my people. Look around you and see beyond your swords, your shields and your talk of war. Open your eyes and you will see that the common people are preparing for Beltane, a druidic festival dressed up in Roman clothes. Take note that the Roman Church does not complain at that. Our lives are full of the old ways. All of our festivals and rituals are based on the old ways. Furthermore, who amongst you would deny praying, at some dark moment, to druidic gods?'

With his face turning puce in indignation Vortipor said: 'There is only one true God, there is only one true faith. There is only one place where prayers should be heard and that is within the walls of a Roman church. Eleri should be condemned for her words and her actions. Arthur was with her, which means that Arthur's claim to the title of Pendragon is void. The Saxons worship Woden and the pagan gods and the Saxons are our enemies. Belief in the old ways and the old superstitions is what we are fighting. With Pasgen murdered, I should become Pendragon!'

'You have a claim to the title,' Cadwallon Longhand said calmly, a hint of superiority playing around his elongated, slender features. 'However,' he added, 'you forget the might of Gwynedd and the power of my teulu. If Pasgen has been murdered by Eleri then I should become Pendragon.'

Rising to his feet, Caradog Strong-arm scowled across the table at Vortipor and Cadwallon. Instinctively, the old warrior's hand went to his sword and his fingers rested upon its hilt as he challenged the noble leaders: 'I bid that you should take care with your words, my lords Vortipor and Cadwallon. We have no proof that Pasgen has been murdered. We should pause and seek the truth and not proceed until Pasgen has been found.'

'I will find the truth and I will warm my hands upon Eleri's flames at the feast to celebrate my accession,' Vortipor said confidently.

'What say you to that?' Ambrosius asked of Eleri. 'Defend yourself; where is Pasgen?'

'I will say nothing in my defence,' Eleri offered, her voice small compared to the ardour of Vortipor's plea and the gravitas of Ambrosius' tone. 'I will say nothing,' Eleri repeated, 'except that I am innocent. I have not met with Pasgen and I have no knowledge of such spells that would make a man disappear.'

Pausing, Ambrosius stared impassively at Eleri, his granite-hard features betraying no emotion, no hint of his deepest thoughts. A warrior from the day he was born, he had been ruthless in his youth and determined that nothing would corrupt his one true aim: victory over the Saxons. Moreover, with the war at its height, would he divert from that path now? All those gathered at the Round Table sat in expectation, awaiting his judgement.

'We have no proof either way and so, on that matter, Eleri's word must be accepted, for now,' Ambrosius reasoned. 'But, if Pasgen cannot be found or if he does not reappear, then this council has the power to decide this noble lady's fate.' Slowly Ambrosius rose to his feet. Then, he beckoned a servant towards the table. 'I suggest that we all leave and make enquiries about Pasgen. For now, Eleri should remain secure within the villa.'

As the servant moved forward to escort Eleri to her room, she glanced across the table at Arthur. The look in her eyes, a beseeching, pleading look, disturbed him. He sensed a vulnerability that had not been present before and, furthermore, he sensed that the Fates were conspiring against him. A question forced itself to the front of Arthur's mind: should he speak up for Eleri and risk the prospect of civil war or should he sacrifice her in the name of unity? His battle-hardened mind told him that he had no choice in the matter. His heart, however, insisted that he should respond to the lady's distress and risk the prospect of conflict.

'We will talk further,' Ambrosius said to Arthur and Dyfrig. 'In private,' he added when Cadwallon, Vortipor and Caradog showed reluctance to leave the room. Eventually, the tribal leaders dragged themselves away from the Round Table, a look of suspicion evident in their eyes, the prospect of conflict apparent within their scowls. Furthermore, when the tribal leaders had finally taken their leave, Ambrosius nodded at the servant and he escorted Eleri to her lodgings within the villa.

Chapter Eleven

The three remaining men gathered around the table: Arthur, Ambrosius and Archbishop Dyfrig. With his features impassive and his mind apparently deep in thought, Ambrosius sat in silence. Eventually, he broke his reverie. Addressing Archbishop Dyfrig, he said: 'What must we do with Eleri of Ergyng?'

Without hesitation the archbishop replied: 'If she has prayed to druidic gods, then she has broken the law of the land and broken the law of Rome. She must be punished.'

Solemnly, Ambrosius nodded in agreement.

'And what of you, Artorius,' Ambrosius asked, 'do you share her beliefs?'

'I do not,' Arthur said. 'It is true, I accompanied Eleri to the shrine in response to her request and to ensure her support and the support of her people.'

'Then there is no mistake,' Ambrosius reasoned, 'she prays to druidic gods.'

'She does,' Arthur confirmed. 'She told me openly that she worships the ancestors.'

'Then you must renounce her,' Ambrosius insisted. 'Furthermore, having no choice, you must condemn Eleri and her beliefs.'

'And bring about a conflict with Ergyng?'

'Better a conflict with Ergyng than a conflict with God,' Ambrosius said. 'If the people of Ergyng decide to rise against us, then we will be victorious, for Ergyng is a small kingdom already ravaged by Saxon incursions. We have no need to worry about the 'might' of Ergyng.'

'Ambrosius speaks the truth,' Dyfrig added. 'You must heed his words.'

'I do not doubt Ambrosius' wisdom,' Arthur said, 'but, with respect, I would state that conflict with Ergyng risks the possibility that they might ally with the Saxons.'

'That is a chance we must take,' Ambrosius said. 'You must condemn Eleri and all who worship the druids.'

'Again,' Arthur persisted, 'with respect, I state that I am not the man for such a task.'

'Why do you utter such words?' Dyfrig demanded. 'Why not obey this simple command? Has she cast a spell on you?' Sadly, the archbishop shook his head. His pained expression gave way to a look of determination as he glared at Arthur. 'You must condemn her,' he said, 'or you will never become Pendragon.'

Arthur knew that the archbishop was a man of his word. Moreover, Ambrosius sought the archbishop's counsel and he placed great faith in the holy man's opinion. If Dyfrig stated that Arthur should not become Pendragon then Ambrosius would adopt his word as law.

'Arthur, reflect well upon our words,' Ambrosius reasoned. 'You are our past, our present and our future, the only man who can unite us. If you do not become Pendragon, our country will see a bloody civil war, a war that will hand victory to the Saxons. Reflect on that before offering any further pronouncements. Accept that we must sacrifice Eleri for the greater good of us all.'

'Allow me to talk with Eleri,' Arthur said, his nimble mind seeking a solution, but finding few possibilities. 'Maybe I can guide her back along the path of Christian faith.'

Thoughtfully, Ambrosius turned to face Archbishop Dyfrig. The moment lingered into an age as the archbishop contemplated Arthur's words. Finally, Dyfrig nodded slowly, offering his blessing.

'Talk with Eleri,' Ambrosius said. 'Return her to the Christian fold. However,' he added, 'your words will fall like seeds upon stone if Pasgen cannot be found.'

'I will find Pasgen,' Arthur said.

'Then go to your task. Bring Pasgen to us and put aside the prospect of civil war and such a nightmare. Allow me to retire to Mynydd-y-Gaer. Allow me to spend the winter of my days in peace.

Then stand tall as Pendragon and lead our people to victory. Defeat the Saxons; bring an end to all conflict. Allow every man, woman and child in this land to savour the reality of peace.'

Chapter Twelve

Arthur stepped into the villa courtyard and the sunlight. There, he found Bedwyr and Cai standing beside the stables. Apparently, they had been sharing a joke, for there was a broad smile upon Bedwyr's handsome face while the suggestion of amusement twinkled in Cai's one dependable chestnut coloured eye. Arthur approached his companions and their faces became sombre as they sensed the task ahead.

'Bedwyr,' Arthur instructed, 'journey to every settlement within riding distance. Question everyone about Pasgen. Ask the people if they have seen him within the past few days. Hopefully, someone will have encountered him or have word of him and he will be found alive.'

Without hesitation Bedwyr nodded. Then he entered the stables and untethered his horse. Meanwhile, Arthur placed a hand upon Cai's shoulder, guiding him towards the stables and his tethered horse.

'Cai,' Arthur said, 'gather together the teulu. Search every woodland and wild area within walking distance. Perform your task well, but pray that you will be unsuccessful, for if you do find

Pasgen in such a wild place then I fear that you will discover him dead.'

'And what of you,' Bedwyr asked from his position astride his horse, 'where will you search?'

'First, I will have words with Eleri. Then, I will join you on your quest.'

As Bedwyr and Cai rode into the distance Arthur retraced his steps back to the villa. He walked through the entrance and beyond the rooms allocated to Marc of Dumnonia, Vortipor and Pasgen. Then, he entered the reception room and the inner courtyard. The guest rooms were to his left with Eleri's room situated between a cubicle set aside for Caradog and a further chamber occupied by Cadwallon. A guard stood beside Eleri's door and he duly stepped aside to allow Arthur entrance.

In keeping with the rest of the villa, the guest room was brightly decorated in vivid reds and vibrant greens with cream borders offering an element of contrast. The floor was covered with an intricate mosaic depicting Venus while the furniture within the room included a cupboard complete with a pitcher and a wooden bowl, a wooden chest and a couch. The couch possessed ornately carved legs and a woollen mattress. Arthur found Eleri reclining on that mattress, her head resting upon a leather cushion.

On catching sight of Arthur, Eleri moved away from the couch. She stood beside the cupboard, offering Arthur her shoulder, while her fingers played with the fringe of her mantle, tugging at its threads.

'I am sorry,' Eleri said.

'You are sorry?' Arthur said. 'Sorry for what reason?'

'For burdening you with so many woes.'

'You can rest easy on that matter, lady, for I went to the spring of my own accord.'

'Then you understand my beliefs?'

'I understand your commitment to your beliefs, but as for the beliefs themselves…they remain a mystery to me.'

'Then allow me to enlighten you,' Eleri said with a hint of optimism creeping into her voice.

Arthur paused. Enlightenment sounded as welcoming as a warm hearth fire on a cold winter's night. Nevertheless, Ambrosius and Dyfrig had spoken and Arthur sensed that the twisted threads of belief were in danger of forming a rope, a rope that others would readily shape into a noose to place around his neck.

Sadly, Arthur said: 'If the weight Ambrosius has placed on my shoulders was not so great then I could think of no greater pleasure than to sit here with you, listening to your words. However, I fear that you must listen to my words and I ask that you do not think ill of me for what I have to say to you.'

'I will not think ill of you,' Eleri responded. 'Indeed, I offer you my respect.'

'If that is so, then for my sake, for your sake, for the sake of all, renounce your beliefs before the Round Table. Should you do so, you will not only save yourself but you will also save your people.'

'I cannot do that,' Eleri replied firmly, a hint of anger distorting her voice, her fists knotting into tight balls as she demonstrated her frustration and her determination. 'I cannot turn my back on my kith and kin. Druidic beliefs are not evil; they are time-honoured beliefs. Our people have embraced these beliefs for generations, for years, time out of mind, long before the Romans came. I cannot renounce my beliefs and I will not forsake my ancestors.'

'And what of God?' Arthur asked calmly. 'Turn to God; He will help you; He will place you on the path to your ancestors.'

'I prayed to God, but I found no solace there.'

Eleri's words cut through Arthur like the bite of a Saxon axe forcing him to grimace. He could understand her words all too clearly, for he had offered prayers to God in the tradition of his parents and in the tradition of Ambrosius and Dyfrig only to find no solace there; no peace, no shaft of wisdom, no enlightenment. Nevertheless, he kept on praying. For what reason? For fear that God would abandon his people and favour the Saxons? Dyfrig spoke of the God of love, but in truth was He the God of fear?

'The laws of Ambrosius state that we must follow the ways of the Roman church,' Arthur said, although even to his own ears his words lacked a sense of conviction.

'Despite the fact that Rome no longer believes in us? Rome has sent no money, no troops since the days of our great-grandfathers; no Roman buildings have been built within our memory. All things Roman - buildings, traditions, beliefs - are crumbling all around us.'

'You speak the truth,' Arthur conceded, 'but I would remind you that this is what we are fighting to rebuild.'

'Then your fight is a hollow fight. Men are sacrificed on Rome's altar with no reward in turn; and Caesar accused the druids of sacrifice!'

The villa walls were substantial, certainly more substantial than the wattle and daub of a roundhouse. Nevertheless, voices carried through the villa walls and Arthur sensed that his enemies would delight in hearing an argument and that they would use words spoken in the heat of the moment or in haste as weapons against him. It was prudent to say no more, he reasoned, and resume the debate when minds were clearer and passions were cooler. When the battle was going against you, it was tempting to rush headlong into the mêlée and lash out in all directions and yet victory was often obtained by regrouping and by calmly stepping back.

'Your words are fine,' Arthur said, 'but they will not forge a key to unlock any door. Only the presence of Pasgen standing within this villa can do that. So, where is Pasgen?'

'I have no idea,' Eleri said. She shook her head then unclenching her fists she allowed her shoulders to drop. With her head bowed, she returned to the couch. 'I have not seen Pasgen since the first Round Table.'

'If Pasgen cannot be found, you will be condemned. Your beliefs will be tested to the full.'

Sitting on the couch Eleri looked up at Arthur through weary eyes, through eyes that had seen too much suffering, too much anguish, too many dreams slaughtered.

'What am I to do?' she sighed.

'Renounce your beliefs.'

'I cannot do that. Without my beliefs I have no peace of mind and without peace in my mind I have no future, no prospect of life.'

'I cannot accept that,' Arthur said. 'For your sake, for my sake, you must renounce your beliefs. The future of our people could well rest on your decision. Think about your people. Think about yourself. Think about us.'

Chapter Thirteen

The following morning Arthur met Bedwyr and Cai at the villa. His search for Pasgen had been in vain and he was beginning to fear that the Lord of Powys would not be found when Bedwyr approached with a smile on his face.

'Maybe Pasgen has been hiding underneath our noses all this time,' Bedwyr said.

'How could this be so?' Arthur asked. 'You have word of him?'

'This morning a guard informed me that Pasgen had been seen, talking with Cerdic.'

Arthur glanced to his right and his eyes caught sight of the building situated at the front of the courtyard, in the right-hand corner, a building that served as a prison.

'You have my gratitude,' Arthur said. 'It is time for words with Cerdic.'

After the guard had unlocked the door Arthur found Cerdic sitting upon a thin mattress in the corner of the prison. The mattress was the only item of furniture within the building. Cerdic glanced up at Arthur, his swarthy features illuminated by a slender shaft of light, a beam that penetrated a high, narrow window.

With a surly look upon his face, Cerdic held up his arms displaying the chains that manacled his wrists together.

'I have not come to release you,' Arthur said, 'although, if you talk and if you are honest with me then I might offer you a moment of freedom from this prison.'

'I have nothing to say,' Cerdic growled, his eyes gazing down to the ground.

Arthur noted that Cerdic's mouth was still discoloured and badly bruised and that the deep gash upon his left arm was proving slow to heal.

'Your arm should be tended,' Arthur said. 'Talk with me and I will instruct our herbalist to apply a poultice of comfrey leaves and roots.'

'I have nothing to say,' Cerdic repeated.

'Such gratitude,' Arthur said sarcastically, his right shoulder leaning comfortably against the wall, his arms folded easily across his chest. 'And to think that I could have allowed Cai to claim your head.'

'How is your knee?' Cerdic spat in reply. 'Had I not slipped upon the wet ground I would have killed you.'

'Maybe,' Arthur said, 'but you lack the skill and the finesse of a noble warrior. And the same can be said of your war band. You will never defeat us.'

Cerdic turned his head away from Arthur, the snarl upon his face displaying his anger, the clenching of his fists and the stretching of his chains displaying his frustration. Apparently defeated he sat, slumped in a dark, damp corner.

From his position beside the door, Arthur waited in silence. He was content to allow the moment to linger, content to allow Cerdic to comprehend his position and his lack of options.

Eventually, Arthur said: 'Pasgen has disappeared. Have you seen him?'

Arthur's words brought a smile to Cerdic's face, his grin revealing crooked and fractured teeth. 'So,' he said, 'the disharmony has begun; events are proving me right. A new Pendragon will not be agreed upon. The tribes will remain divided and my Saxon friends will defeat them one-by-one. And we must not forget the Picts and the Irish; maybe they will side with the Saxons. Then the Britons will be slaughtered: every man, woman and child.'

'True,' Arthur agreed, 'we must not forget the Picts and the Irish, but we must also remember that the Irish are at peace with us now.'

'That may be so, but the Irish and the Picts are watching and as soon as they sense a weakness they will invade. If you were a wise man, you would swear allegiance to Aelle.'

'If that is your definition of wisdom,' Arthur said, 'then I thank God that I am a simple man.'

Throwing his head back Cerdic laughed, a laugh that shook his shoulders and jangled his wrist chains. 'You have spent too long in Ambrosius' company,' he said.

'Ambrosius is a good man,' Arthur said calmly. 'His name stands for loyalty, for truth and for justice.'

'Ambrosius is a Roman and what has Rome brought to the Britons? Plagues, wars, famines. Better to place your faith elsewhere, in a god that offers protection, not persecution. Pray to the Saxon god, Woden.'

As Cerdic spoke, he took hold of an old Roman coin, a pendant that hung around his neck. It served as a talisman to ward off evil spirits. The coin had no material value and its origin was unimportant. However, the belief that the coin offered protection was real in the mind of Cerdic and his followers.

'Woden is the god of war,' Arthur replied. 'He brings nothing but death and destruction.'

'And the god of Rome is the god of peace?' Again Cerdic laughed, his shoulders shaking in mock amusement. 'Look around you. Look at your scars. Are they badges of peace?'

'My scars are badges of war and I would sooner lose all faith than submit to Woden.'

While Arthur could accept, though not fully understand, Eleri and her belief in the ancestors, he could not accept the Saxons and their belief in Woden, for Woden had brought devastation and ruin to his homeland. In Arthur's mind, Woden was the Devil, a source of evil and his people would only find peace when that evil had been defeated.

'You met with Pasgen,' Arthur said. 'What did you discuss?'

'I did not meet with Pasgen,' Cerdic snarled. 'No conversation took place.'

'You were seen,' Arthur insisted. 'The guards allowed Pasgen entry.'

From his position slumped against the prison wall, Cerdic glanced up at Arthur, peering at him from the corner of his right eye. Eventually, he conceded that he could no longer withhold the truth and so, with a shrug, he said: 'We discussed possible unions and treaties should Pasgen become Pendragon.'

'That looks unlikely now.'

'Maybe,' Cerdic mumbled.

'Did you kill Pasgen?'

'How?' Cerdic's head jerked to the right in a show of anger. Climbing to his feet, he held out his hands displaying his shackles and wrists, made dirty by the rusty chain. 'I have been locked up in here,' he snapped bitterly, surveying the four damp walls. 'Besides, Pasgen talked of a possible union. With Pasgen as Pendragon, I would command even greater respect.'

After careful thought, Arthur concluded that Cerdic was telling the truth. Therefore, the search for Pasgen would continue and while proof of his demise remained absent, a glimmer of hope would linger.

'I will send our herbalist to tend your wounds and allow you a moment in the day to walk around the courtyard under guard,' Arthur said.

'Such generosity,' Cerdic growled, spitting on the ground.

'We are well-known for our kindness,' Arthur smiled. 'Leave us in peace and you can keep the land you have claimed. However, invade Glywysing and you will feel the might of our swords. Invade my homeland and the Saxon leaders will never see their land again.'

Chapter Fourteen

Later that afternoon, as Arthur stood beside the river outside the villa, a ship approached from the east. At first, he was surprised for the vessel was already in shallow water. The day was clear, the sea was calm and therefore the sentries should have called attention to the ship as it sailed across the open sea. In times of strife such lapses were beyond forgiveness and so Arthur would have words with the sentries and remind them of their duty.

For now, Arthur watched as the ship, a flat-bottomed vessel with a high bow and a high stern, made its way towards the mouth of the river. Sails constructed from raw hides billowed in the favourable breeze, powering the vessel along the river towards the villa. Arthur recognised the vessel as belonging to Marc of Dumnonia, for Marc favoured ships that were carved from oak. The hull was supported by cross-timbers, which in turn were secured by iron bolts. As the ship approached the villa, members of Marc's teulu lowered its sails. Then they unfurled a heavy iron chain and hurled an anchor into the water.

The first person to disembark from the ship was Marc of Dumnonia. To Arthur's surprise, his former lover, Gwenhwyfar of Powys, followed

Marc on to the riverbank. Arthur took a moment to study Gwenhwyfar and he concluded that she had lost none of her beauty. Unusually for a Briton Gwenhwyfar had golden hair, curling about her shoulders; also, she had emerald-green eyes, snow-white skin, crimson lips and regular, even teeth. Her cheekbones were high and her smile graceful. Her legs were long and slender and her hips were gently curved. Her waist was slim and her breasts were generous. She wore a variegated woollen gown, predominantly brown in colour, while her under tunic was long with close-fitting sleeves and a V-shaped neckline. A long shawl hung from her shoulders, a delicate leather belt encircled her slender waist and a pair of finely crafted leather shoes graced her feet. As Gwenhwyfar walked beyond Arthur, without glancing in his direction, she exuded an air of confidence, a sense of importance and the belief that she had been born to grace a nobleman's hall.

Gwenhwyfar entered the villa courtyard, ignoring her sister, Morganna, who was standing beside the main gate. 'Let her go', Arthur said to himself, although a faint voice whispered in his ear, suggesting that he should give chase.

As Gwenhwyfar entered the villa, Arthur turned his attention to the ship and Marc of Dumnonia. Marc was also known as Cunomorus and Cynfawr, the Hound of the Sea. He held lands across the eastern sea, on the mainland of Armorica. Although his enemies would point to his large ears and mock him, Marc had handsome, even features, light-brown eyes and chestnut coloured hair. His hair reached his collar, framing a face unblemished by battle. His chin carried a dark stubble and the suggestion of a dimple. His shoulders were broad, his muscles were well toned and he stood well above average height.

Marc wore a short blue-dyed tunic, with sleeves protruding below a protective covering of chainmail. His breeches were made of linen, while his laced shoes were crafted from fine leather. In addition a fur cloak, complete with a bronze brooch, hung from his shoulders, while a battle-scarred iron sword hung from his belt. In battle, he wore a close-fitting headpiece. Lined with leather, the iron headpiece was adorned with a crest featuring a snarling horse. Strangely, Marc appeared reticent, reluctant to step forward. Eventually, he grinned and that familiar grin compelled Arthur to walk towards his friend.

'She found her way to my door,' Marc said, defensively, his gaze following the path taken by Gwenhwyfar. 'I hope this will not sour the honey of our friendship.'

Arthur paused as he recalled a moment upon the battlefield, an encounter with the Saxons at the River Bassas, a river that bordered Marc's territory. Upon that day, the Saxons had threatened to gain an advantage and claim Arthur's life in the process. However, Marc had intervened and Arthur's life had been saved. Such moments lived long in the memory and those moments forged a friendship, a kinship and a bond of mutual trust that, like a well-made sword, was difficult to break.

'Gwenhwyfar left my side a long time ago,' Arthur replied. He sighed: 'I wish you good luck; I think you will need it.'

Marc laughed. Then he opened his arms, inviting an embrace, an embrace that Arthur accepted. Thus, the bond of friendship was reaffirmed.

'What took you so long?' Arthur asked as the two men walked towards the villa.

'I had to secure the eastern border of Dumnonia and after that the winds were against us when we tried to set sail. And what of you?' Marc enquired, his words directed at Arthur while his eyes scrutinised the coastline. 'In my absence, what joys and troubles have accompanied you, my friend?'

Arthur followed Marc's gaze out to sea. Apart from the waves breaking gently upon the shoreline, there was little to capture his attention.

'Ambrosius nominated me as Pendragon,' Arthur said.

'Then I offer you my heartfelt congratulations,' Marc smiled, his gesture revealing that one of his front teeth had been damaged upon a piece of quernstone, a rogue fragment that had found its way into a loaf of bread.

'You will swear allegiance to me?' Arthur probed.

'Indeed, I will.'

'Then our cause is strengthened.' Arthur was about to mirror Marc's smile, when thoughts of Eleri forced his facial muscles into a frown. 'However, there remains a problem; Pasgen has disappeared.'

'Murdered?' Marc said.

'Possibly. Eleri of Ergyng has been accused. The tribal leaders say that she made Pasgen disappear through the use of druidic spells.'

Unperturbed, Marc offered Arthur his winning smile: 'If Pasgen has disappeared,' Marc said, 'then Eleri should be congratulated. Perchance she will cast the same spell upon Vortipor and Cadwallon!'

'Eleri is innocent,' Arthur rebuked stoically.

'And doubtless all will agree when Pasgen has been found.'

Once again, Marc cast his gaze out to sea and, instinctively, Arthur followed his line of sight. Now, light clouds were rolling in with the tide and fishing boats were making their way towards the villa. A child ran joyfully across the beach. The scene offered Arthur a moment of contentment, a moment of peace.

'But tell me,' Marc said, resuming his stroll towards the villa, 'what of the Saxons; what of their threat?'

'We confronted Cerdic and his war band at the stepping-stones river. The war band was defeated and Cerdic was captured.'

Marc frowned, his stride faltering as he expressed concern. 'Has Cerdic said anything to explain his presence this far west?'

'Not a word. Cerdic holds his tongue.'

'I would like words with Cerdic.'

'That can be arranged,' Arthur confirmed.

The two men walked in silence until they found themselves within the villa, standing in the garden, opposite the guest rooms. Marc gazed at his surroundings, nodding with approval at the ornate columns and the four-square villa walls.

'And what of Arthur?' Marc asked absently, his gaze remaining somewhat distant, his thoughts clearly preoccupied, lost within his surroundings. 'You're in rude health?' Without waiting for a reply, he continued: 'As you can probably see I have found a measure of contentment and that contentment coincided with the day Gwenhwyfar arrived at my door.'

'And what of your wife, Essyllt?' Arthur said, sotto voce.

'A boil to be lanced,' Marc said, his languid tone suggesting that the matter was beneath his contempt. 'I will obtain a divorce. Dyfrig and his Church will oppose me and scream all manner of hell, but I will offer them a gift of some land and the problem will be solved.'

Then, from one of the guest rooms Gwenhwyfar appeared and the smile returned to Marc's face.

'We will talk later,' Marc of Dumnonia said. 'For now, I must warm myself upon the flames of love and tend to Gwenhwyfar's needs.'

Chapter Fifteen

Morganna viewed the arrival of Marc's vessel with a sense of malevolent amusement. She was tempted to laugh when she caught sight of her sister, Gwenhwyfar, but she suppressed that feeling. Instead, she contented herself with an amused smile and a plethora of wicked thoughts.

As Gwenhwyfar strode haughtily towards the villa, Morganna recalled their youth and the days when Gwenhwyfar was far from noble and demure. Her sister should have committed her body and soul to Arthur and in return she would have received wealth, comfort and love. However, Gwenhwyfar wanted more; more wealth, greater comfort and a man who would worship her as Dyfrig worshipped his god, and for that reason alone Morganna knew that Gwenhwyfar would be eternally disappointed.

Morganna stepped back into the shadows and allowed Gwenhwyfar to enter the villa. They had no words to exchange and any conversation between them would have been poisoned by oaths of spite. Therefore, it was better to retain a measure of decorum and maintain a dignified silence.

As Gwenhwyfar sought the comforts of the villa, Morganna turned her attention to Arthur and

Marc. Marc was a handsome man, she had to confess and even though she did not trust him, she would still invite him to warm her bed. However, she would enjoy the moment and hold no great expectations for the future. She would take what was on offer and allow the devil to claim the rest.

All the talk around the villa had been about her husband: had anyone seen Pasgen? Arthur's men were running around in circles looking for him, yet Morganna knew that they would not find him, at least not alive, for she had witnessed Pasgen's murder from her place in the shadows. Morganna knew who was responsible. Even so, she would not speak out. There was a game to play, rewards to be won, especially from Arthur.

The man who was destined to become the new Pendragon stood alone in the villa garden; now was Morganna's chance to talk to him, now was the moment to instigate her plan.

'You appear perplexed,' Morganna remarked as she walked alongside Arthur. 'You appear troubled; please allow me to offer my assistance.'

Arthur paused. He allowed his gaze to wander over Morganna. Was he admiring her long, dark, flowing hair, her seductive eyes, her firm breasts, her slender waist, which continued to hide the developing child, or was he trying to peer into the devious depths of her mind?

'You could assist me greatly,' Arthur replied. 'All that I ask is that you help me to locate your husband.'

'Willingly, I will do that,' Morganna lied.

Arthur nodded, as if satisfied. He resumed his stroll towards the courtyard, his gaze fixed on Morganna, his mind apparently oblivious of Cadwallon and Vortipor as they looked on from the main gate.

'When was the last time you saw Pasgen?' Arthur asked.

'After the Round Table, that night, when he went to bed,' Morganna lied. 'He appeared in good spirits, convinced that he would become Pendragon.'

'Did he leave his bed during the night?'

'On that matter, I do not know,' she sighed. Then, after a pause: 'For we do not sleep together.'

In a dramatic show of emotion, Morganna buried her face in her hands. Her shoulders shook uncontrollably as tears ran down her cheeks. She sobbed loudly, attracting the attention of Vortipor's band of warriors.

'I fear the worst,' Morganna cried. 'I fear that Pasgen has been murdered. It would appear that I am a widow. I have no man to protect me.'

'You will have no trouble in finding another man,' Arthur reasoned, his gaze leaving Morganna and wandering to the wooded area to the east of the villa compound, to the site of the druidic spring.

'But will he be the right man? I want someone brave, someone noble, someone honourable. I want you, Arthur.'

'You have misplaced your affections,' Arthur said coldly. 'I am not for you.'

'And I am not for you? Not even if I can help you to save Eleri.'

'If you know anything about Pasgen's disappearance, you should talk now,' Arthur insisted.

'If I talk,' Morganna said, her fingers wiping away the tears from underneath her eyes, 'I fear revenge.'

'If you talk I will assign Cai to watch over you. Then, you need not fear anyone or anything.'

'Cai is a brave man.'

'He is,' Arthur agreed.

'But you are braver,' Morganna insisted. 'I want you to watch over me,' she implored, 'every day and every night.'

Arthur shook his head and the suggestion of a smile brightened his face, the gleam in his eye demonstrating that he understood the game Morganna was trying to play.

Once more, Arthur glanced towards the woodland and the druidic spring. 'I must leave you,' he said. 'However, before I go I suggest that you should take my advice: save your words for someone who is more deserving.'

'Wait!' Morganna yelled as she gathered up her purple cloak and ran after Arthur. His determined stride had taken him on to the woodland path, away from the villa, and he had travelled some distance along that path before Morganna caught up with him. After pausing, to allow her hand to caress her womb, to soothe the developing foetus and return her body to a sense of calm, she said: 'I will go away and search the recesses of my mind. In turn, I suggest that you should think also. Think carefully about my offer. I have gazed into the future and I have seen that there is only one way to save Eleri. There is only one way to keep her alive, and that is with you at my side.'

Chapter Sixteen

Leaving Morganna and her schemes behind, Arthur followed the path through the ferns until he arrived at the river. He was convinced that Morganna knew more about Pasgen and his whereabouts than she was willing to reveal but, short of torture or yielding to her plans, he could think of no solution. Maybe the druidic spring would offer enlightenment. Arthur was not sure why he felt compelled to walk to the spring, but something beyond his understanding told him that he should go there.

Arthur entered the area of dense woodland, which was rich and verdant with tall oak trees. Then, stepping down into the hollow, he knelt beside the spring. As the water bubbled up through a fissure in the limestone, he peered into the spring to view his ancestors. However, just as before, he saw nothing, he experienced no mystical sensation. Frowning, he judged that his lack of belief in the ancestors precluded all hope of enlightenment.

The sudden sound of a snapping twig ended Arthur's period of quiet reflection. Alert, he reached for his sword. He was about to unsheathe Caledfwlch when he caught sight of a tall man possessing a lean and muscular frame. In addition, the man had a broad forehead and long unkempt hair, oaken in colour, a tone matched by his straggling goatee beard. His eyes were hazel, as calm as they were thoughtful while his nose was long and slender, noble upon prominent cheekbones. He wore a birrus, a hooded coat, over an ankle-length tunic. Both the coat and the tunic were a faded green in colour. Around his waist, there hung a leather belt complete with an antler belt-buckle and a bone-handled dagger. Simple leather boots covered his feet while, in his right hand, there rested a wooden staff adorned with a goat's skull. A charm, in the shape of a phallus, hung around his neck. Arthur formed the opinion that this man was as organic as the forest, that his limbs were an extension of roots within the soil.

'Who are you?' Arthur asked, his hand relaxing and parting company with his sword. 'What are you doing here?'

'This is my place,' the man said. 'Along with my people I am barred from your settlements and your hill forts; we must make our home in the forest.'

'You are a druid?'

'I am,' the man smiled. 'I venerate the ancestors. They offer me wisdom, they offer me peace.'

'And what of Rome,' Arthur asked, 'what of the Christian god?'

'Rome...' The forest man paused. After clearing a path with his staff, he made his way through the undergrowth and sat upon a rock beside the spring. 'Over many years,' he continued, 'the Romans stole from us and then they abandoned us, but not before they had killed the last of us, or so they thought. To add insult to our wounds, they also destroyed our sacred groves and desecrated our places of worship. Until my dying day I will contend that Rome is not an ideal to aspire to.'

'I have been told of this,' Arthur admitted, 'by the people of Badon, though not by my teachers. How do you know that this story is not a myth? How do I know that you speak the truth?'

'Such knowledge has been handed down through the generations,' the forest man said, his fingers caressing the goat's skull. 'The ancestors do not lie; I speak the truth.'

'I cannot believe that Rome contained so much evil,' Arthur said. 'You must be mistaken; how could so much evil emanate from the words of Christ?'

While glaring at Arthur, the forest man shook his head in vigorous fashion. 'There is no mistake. My ancestors carried the scars of Rome to their graves. As for the words of Christ...he spoke for the common people, but men in power manipulated his words and now those men perpetrate the greatest sin of all, they conduct their iniquity not under the cover of darkness, but in the full glare of sunlight under the cover of Christ's name.'

'Your words suggest that you should find a home with the Saxons,' Arthur reasoned.

'My words suggest nothing of the sort. The Saxons seek war and land, without consideration for the people or our ancestors. We seek peace and knowledge and we respect the land, the land that provides us with food and shelter. You have cast us into the wilderness; the Saxons would cast us into the ground.'

Arthur nodded, demonstrating a level of understanding. 'So,' he surmised, 'you would not find a home amongst the Saxons and yet you would abandon Rome and Christian beliefs?'

'I remind you again, Rome abandoned us. Even so, if we are to find peace, with each other, with the Saxons, then we must learn to tolerate and accept individual beliefs. All men and all beliefs are essential to make this land strong.'

The forest man paused, his gaze wandering to the spring. Like Eleri before him, the water appeared to hold him in a trance. In the tranquillity of the moment, Arthur took time to reflect upon the forest man's words. Although he felt restricted by the laws as determined by Ambrosius and the demands of the Roman Church he could appreciate the ideals as expressed by his companion. However, ideals and reality were often as far apart as peace and harmony between the Britons and the Saxons and, within that moment, Arthur could not visualise the material with which to build a bridge.

Turning his attention back to Arthur, the forest man continued: 'Belief is a powerful force and belief can be a force for good. However, belief has to come from the heart, not won by the sword; let the people decide for themselves. Rome was too afraid of the people; Rome would not allow them to find a path to salvation and so they destroyed all paths, except the path that led to the Christian god. The Romans persecuted and murdered my people. The Romans replaced our shrines and our festivals with their temples and their rituals. The Romans feared our knowledge. The Romans feared us; they feared what they did not understand. Furthermore, they made no attempt to seek understanding. Rome sought to impose its will, and yet the path to peace is lined with tolerance and compassion.'

With a smile cracking through his hirsute features the forest man placed his staff upon the ground and using that staff as a lever, he eased himself to his feet. Standing tall, he walked over to Arthur. As the two men faced each other, Arthur realised that the forest man had not asked his name and yet Arthur sensed that this man knew who stood before him. Arthur also sensed that this man possessed a great store of wisdom, possibly a store of wisdom in excess of the knowledge accumulated at Illtud's monastery.

'If I may,' the forest man enquired, 'I would like to ask you a question: what are you doing in our forest?'

'I am looking for a noble lord called Pasgen.'

'Describe this man.'

'Pasgen has long hair, grey in colour. He wears a beard and a striped tunic. He carries his sword over his right shoulder. His nose is misshapen and his face betrays the passing of many seasons. Have you seen this man within the forest?'

'I saw someone resembling that description,' the forest man admitted.

'When?' Arthur asked.

'About two or three moons ago.'

'Where?'

'Over there.' The forest man raised his staff and pointed towards a clearing, a glade that led to the river.

'Pasgen entered the forest alone?'

'No, he did not,' the forest man replied, 'the man had a companion.'

'Describe his companion.'

'It was dark.' The forest man shrugged in apologetic fashion. 'My back was turned. I did not linger, but I went about my business.'

'What is your business?' Arthur frowned.

'I study the stars; I study their place in the world of the ancestors and the omens they foretell.'

'And what do the stars foretell?'

'They suggest that there will be a mighty battle between the Britons and the Saxons and that battle will decide the future of this land.'

'Will the Britons be victorious?' Arthur asked eagerly.

After a brief pause, the forest man smiled, revealing even, white teeth: 'That, the stars do not foretell.'

'Thank you for your words and wisdom,' Arthur said, his gaze and mind wandering to the glade and the river.

'My wisdom stems from my beliefs,' the forest man said, 'whereas my words are free, unlike my people.'

Arthur paused and waited while the forest man made his way into the depths of the forest. Although his attention and gaze remained fixed upon the forest man, he could not determine the moment when that man disappeared into the trees. Indeed the man appeared to blend into the forest and become at one with his surroundings.

Placing all thoughts of the forest man to the back of his mind Arthur made his way through the glade. Arriving at the river, he glanced along the curved bank, his gaze wandering to a tree, which flourished beside the water. Arthur walked over to the tree where he discovered, caught upon a branch, threads of striped linen. Were they fragments from Pasgen's tunic? Squatting beside the riverbank Arthur noticed that the mud had been disturbed and that heavy footprints remained, embedded in the damp soil. Arthur followed those footprints until they disappeared into the ferns. Crouching, he brushed the ferns to one side. Then, he noticed two scars upon the ground, two parallel lines that continued into the depths of the ferns. Arthur followed the lines until his right boot struck something solid. Glancing down he caught sight of a human body. From his experience on the battlefield, Arthur knew that this man was dead. Indeed, it appeared as though someone had struck him about the head, repeatedly, leaving a mask of congealed blood upon his face. Despite the bloody mask, the swollen features and splintered skull, Arthur recognised the man and he sighed when he realised that his search for Pasgen was over.

Chapter Seventeen

After making his gruesome discovery, Arthur returned to the villa. There, he instructed Bedwyr to assemble the tribal leaders and escort them to the river. Meanwhile, accompanied by Cai, Arthur revisited the scene of Pasgen's demise.

With the clouds gathering and with daylight yielding to nightfall Arthur collected a pinewood torch from the villa and by the light of that torch, he examined the ground around Pasgen's body. Despite his fingertip search, he found nothing; no object, no item that would incriminate the murderer. While holding the pinewood torch close to Pasgen's face Arthur turned to Cai for his opinion:

'What do you make of this?'

'Clearly, he was murdered.'

'A heavy weapon,' Arthur surmised.

Before replying, Cai allowed his large right hand to caress his thick russet beard as he gave the matter careful thought. Eventually, he nodded and said: 'From the shape of his wounds I would suggest that Pasgen was beaten repeatedly with the pommel of a heavy sword.'

Arthur was about to concur with Cai when the sound of voices and movement within the ferns alerted him to the fact that Bedwyr had arrived, accompanied by Morganna, Archbishop Dyfrig and all the tribal leaders.

At first Morganna was hesitant and she required a guiding hand from Ambrosius before she would move forward. With reluctant tread she approached Pasgen, her hand poised in front of her mouth, as though ready to stifle a scream. In the event her wail of anguish cut through the night air and instead of stifling her yowl, she buried her head in her hands.

Despite the solemnity of the moment, Arthur was moved to reflect on Morganna's behaviour. Questions crowded his mind: did the lady behave in all sincerity? What secrets did she hold? Could she have played a part in Pasgen's murder? While Arthur considered those questions, Ambrosius stepped forward, offering Morganna a firm, supportive hand.

'I am sorry for your loss,' Ambrosius said.

In silence Morganna nodded, her anguish replaced by a look of confusion, a sense that she was lost and, for a brief moment, Arthur felt a pang of sorrow for her, a sensation that faded when he called to mind his doubts about her behaviour and his suspicions regarding her motives.

While Ambrosius comforted Morganna, Vortipor stepped forward to examine Pasgen's body. With a grim look of acceptance upon his face the leader of the Demetians bowed, offering his kinsman due respect. However, when he turned to face Ambrosius, Vortipor's rotund, youthful features took on the colour of his red beard as he displayed his anger:

'You see,' he growled, 'I was right. Now, we claim justice and put Eleri to the flame.'

'Wait!' Caradog insisted. 'We have no proof that Eleri was responsible for this sin.'

'What proof do we need?' Vortipor complained. 'The woman is in league with demonic spirits. It is clear that she carried out this murder so that Arthur could become Pendragon.'

Unconvinced, Caradog Strong-arm adopted a determined, pugnacious expression. Puffing out his barrel-shaped chest, he strode towards Vortipor and the riverbank.

'You overlook several important details,' Caradog stated while studying the scars upon the earth and the disturbance amongst the ferns. 'Pasgen is a long way from his lodgings and these marks upon the ground suggest that he was dragged here after he was murdered. I ask you, how could Eleri drag such a man?'

'She had an accomplice,' Vortipor reasoned.

'Who?' Caradog challenged.

'Obviously Arthur. Arthur and Eleri are in league together.'

'Now you stretch your imagination beyond the horizon,' Caradog said. Placing his right hand upon the hilt of his sword, he took a step towards Vortipor, the anger within his expression offering a challenge. 'Arthur would not murder Pasgen; his honour would forbid such an act.'

In his frustration, Vortipor turned his shoulder towards Caradog. Then, he marched towards the tall oak tree whereupon he confronted Ambrosius. While holding his arms out in beseeching fashion the leader of the Demetians said:

'We talk and grow cold when we should be warming ourselves upon Eleri's flames. Let us see justice done and then let all swear allegiance to me; honour me as Pendragon, for this was Pasgen's greatest wish.'

'No one swears allegiance to any man, at least not until we hear the truth of this matter,' Ambrosius judged.

'Then let us hear the truth,' Vortipor grinned, his features brightening as a hint of devilment danced in his eyes.

'How should we hear the truth?' Cadwallon asked, his long, lean frame stepping out of the silent shadows before joining the tribal leaders assembled beside the riverbank.

'Trial by ordeal,' Vortipor said simply. 'At dawn we place Eleri in the freshwater pool beside the villa. If she rises to the surface, she is guilty, if she remains under the water until the sun reaches its highest point in the sky, she is innocent.'

'We will require the Church to bless such a trial,' Ambrosius said, his gaze falling upon Archbishop Dyfrig.

In the gathering darkness, the flickering flames of Arthur's pinewood torch highlighted Dyfrig's pensive expression. The archbishop took a moment to caress the painful inflammation around the knuckles of his left hand before nodding in affirmation:

'You have the Church's blessing.'

'Therefore we will hold the trial,' Ambrosius said, his tone solemn, his expression grim, 'for a trial is the only fair way to obtain the truth.'

After glancing at the tribal leaders and noting that the majority were nodding in approval, Arthur took a step towards Ambrosius. Although his anger threatened to crush the pinewood torch held tightly in his hand, his voice remained calm and even when he said:

'This cannot be just; think carefully, would Rome approve of our actions?'

'Vortipor's suggestion is sound,' Marc said. With an easy smile upon his face, the leader of the

Dumnonians walked over to Arthur and placed a reassuring hand upon his shoulder. 'Add your voice to the trial and bear witness to the truth.'

'I will not support such barbarity,' Arthur said, his gaze beckoning Bedwyr and Cai. 'Instead, I will search my wits and uncover the truth.'

Growling in frustration, Ambrosius yelled: 'Enough! Take to your beds and rise at dawn; we will gather beside the pool. And with the tribal leaders as witnesses and God as our judge we will resolve this matter once and for all.'

Chapter Eighteen

With Vortipor at her side and with members of her teulu carrying Pasgen's body, Morganna returned to the villa. The teulu would transport Pasgen to Powys and they would bury him in home soil. Morganna knew that she should journey with them. However, first she had to realise her plan and secure a brighter future for herself and her child. As she walked, she caressed her womb and although all around her carried the weight of despair and solemnity, she felt a frisson of excitement, which displayed itself in a smile.

When Morganna arrived at the villa, she found Arthur in the courtyard talking with Bedwyr and Cai. Presently, Arthur dispatched the two men and they faded into the darkness, no doubt with the hope of securing a future for Eleri. Morganna knew that Eleri would not survive the trial by ordeal simply because the noble leaders needed someone to blame for Pasgen's murder. Morganna also knew that Arthur would seek to halt the trial and that his desperation to save Eleri offered her, and her plan, the greatest chance of success.

With her cheeks flushed in excitement, Morganna ran towards Arthur. 'Please,' she said, 'spend time with me this sorrowful night.'

'I feel a great sadness for you and for what has happened to Pasgen,' Arthur said, 'but you must excuse me, I have no time to waste this night.'

'Not even a moment for a widow?' Morganna pleaded. 'I am all alone,' she said in a small, sombre voice. 'I am in need of a husband; have you considered my offer of marriage?'

'I have considered, and there will be no such marriage.'

'Not even to save Eleri?'

The moon cut through the clouds illuminating Arthur's expression. Although that expression remained impassive, Morganna sensed Arthur's anger and hostility. Despite herself, Morganna smiled, for she expected nothing less. Arthur was a great prize and she knew that she would have to fight to claim her reward. And fight she would with the belief that, over time, Arthur would mellow and accept her as his wife.

'If you know the truth about Pasgen's murder,' Arthur said indignantly, 'then you should speak out.'

'I know the truth and I will speak out, after you have agreed to the marriage.'

The scent of pinewood torches drifted on the night air as the breeze cajoled and teased the flames. The aroma was agreeable to Morganna and she could have danced with those flames, danced with

Arthur, all night long. However, she noted that with every hostile word Arthur was wont to glance towards the villa and Eleri's prison.

Turning on his heel, Arthur said: 'Your words are evil, lady, and despite all your conspiracies and schemes, you will never achieve your aims. I will find other means to save Eleri.' Then, with pride and determination in every stride, he marched towards the villa.

'Wait!' Morganna yelled as she gathered up her purple cloak and ran across the courtyard. Arthur was about to enter the villa when she reached out, placing a restraining hand upon his arm. 'It is plain,' she said, 'that you have feelings for Eleri. In truth, that makes me jealous. However, I have feelings of my own; I can understand your love. Nevertheless, I ask you, try to understand me; I am a woman alone, please consider my sorrow. Consider also my greatest wish, which is to experience love. Through all the winters and all the summers of my life, I have been denied love. Please, I beg of you, try to understand how empty that makes me feel.'

'Soon, you will have the love of a child,' Arthur replied, 'surely no woman could ask for more.'

'My child will love me and I will love him,' Morganna agreed, 'but I am in need of a greater love, a love that only a man can offer.'

'Then return to Powys,' Arthur suggested, 'and find such a man.'

In the darkness, Morganna felt the chill of the night air and, as she bit her bottom lip, she pulled her cloak tightly around her shoulders. Arthur was about to enter the villa, he was going to reject her and her plans. Morganna could not allow that to happen. She had to say something, anything, to capture Arthur's attention and compel him to change his mind.

'If I cannot claim happiness for myself,' Morganna pleaded, 'then at least grant this wish for my child; claim him as your own.'

'Why,' Arthur asked, 'for what reason?'

'Soon, you will become Pendragon. The tribal leaders will have no choice; to prevent war amongst the Britons they will have to support you. Even though you are not from a noble house, you have noble qualities; you are brave, compassionate, intelligent. You stand tall; you look down on all their noble heads. Take pity on me; claim my son as your own so that, one day, he will become Pendragon.'

'I cannot do that,' Arthur said while turning his back on Morganna and entering the villa; 'the price is still too high.'

'Then Eleri will burn!' Morganna yelled. 'And for the rest of your days you will live with the knowledge that you kindled the first flame.'

Chapter Nineteen

Darkness crowded the room. Darkness crowded Arthur's thoughts. Within the villa, he paced, first to one wall, then another, as he sought light and a possible solution. He reflected on the forest man and his wisdom; he considered his own beliefs and attitudes towards Rome; he also thought deeply about Morganna and her offer of marriage. After wandering around in circles, both in his room and in his mind, Arthur realised that he was unable to rationalise these myriad thoughts and so he returned to the courtyard and the freshness of the cold night air.

Arthur gazed up at the moon. Full and vivid, a face of wisdom appeared to stare back at him, mocking him in his moment of indecision. A series of sounds, the opening of a villa door and an expletive as someone embraced the cold night air, distracted Arthur. Then, out of the corner of his eye, he caught sight of Caradog's pugnacious outline as the Lord of Gwent ambled across the courtyard.

'I could not sleep either,' Caradog complained while stifling a yawn before drawing a weary hand across his face.

'What are we to do?' Arthur asked, his gaze still fixed on the moon.

'If you were Pendragon, what would you do?'

Arthur glanced at his sword, Caledfwlch. He drew Caledfwlch from its scabbard and he studied the blade, the keeper of his secrets, the brutal source of his wisdom, omniscient in the moonlight.

'If you had asked that question seven moons ago,' Arthur reflected, 'I would have replied: follow the Rule of Rome.'

'And under this moon?' Caradog probed while glancing up at the night sky.

Arthur considered that he should place the tip of Caledfwlch into the ground and then kneel to pray before the cross of the warrior. However, instead he said: 'While looking for Pasgen, I stumbled across a man in the forest, a druid. He told me of murder and destruction, perpetrated in the name of Rome. He offered me words of wisdom and hinted at learning, hinted at knowledge far greater than the teaching at Illtud's monastery. We need such wisdom, we need every weapon at our disposal to defeat the Saxons and bring peace to this land.'

'We need such men and women,' Caradog agreed. 'But we also need the blessing of Dyfrig and his Church.'

'Why must we have one without the other?' Arthur reasoned. 'A man is born with two hands; why must we tie one hand behind our back?'

'I am a simple man,' Caradog shrugged, a smile adding deep lines to his battle-scarred features, 'a man who is easily vexed by such questions. All I understand is the threat posed by the Saxons at my eastern border. If your decision means greater security for my people and a reduced threat along that border, then Caradog Strong-arm will lend you his strength and his sword.'

With a firm, but friendly, thump Caradog Strong-arm struck Arthur upon his back before turning to face the villa. Then, wearily, he ambled towards his bed.

The darkest hour precedes the dawn, so the wise men said. Glancing up Arthur noticed that a ribbon of sunlight had appeared on the horizon, suggesting that the darkest hour was about to end.

With a look of determination upon his face, Arthur returned to the villa. He entered Eleri's room. There, he found the Lady of Ergyng reclining on her mattress, her head resting upon a leather cushion.

'Soon Dyfrig will join us and the trial will begin,' Arthur said.

'I am aware of the trial,' Eleri said, her eyes staring up at the garishly painted ceiling, her fingers tugging restlessly at the fringe of her mantle.

'How are your spirits?'

'They remain strong,' Eleri insisted. Her gaze settled on Arthur and he sensed her resolve and her resilience. He saw the anger, burning in her eyes.

'And what of your beliefs?' Arthur said.

Eleri eased herself away from the couch. She walked over to a cupboard. There, she picked up a pitcher and poured water into a wooden bowl. Gazing into the water, and with her back to Arthur, she said: 'I have no cause to doubt my beliefs.'

'I met with a wise man in the forest,' Arthur said. 'We discussed your beliefs.'

Despite the gravity of the situation, a smile played around Eleri's lips, touching the corners of her dark, soul-searching eyes. 'And so,' she enquired, 'you have moved a step closer to enlightenment?'

'I admit that one thought leads me along that path into sunshine. However, the next thought leads me further into shadow; I can appreciate your beliefs, but what of my beliefs in Rome?' Arthur caressed the hilt of Caledfwlch just as Dyfrig might caress his wooden cross; he sighed: 'I see now that the Roman way holds many flaws, but I cannot abandon my beliefs, I cannot abandon Rome.'

'And so you must abandon me,' Eleri concluded quietly before dipping her fingers into the cold water and drawing those fingers across her eyes.

'I cannot do that either,' Arthur said. 'Equally, I know how precious your beliefs are to you and I realise that I cannot ask you to abandon those beliefs.'

'So,' Eleri enquired tentatively, 'when you become Pendragon, you will allow us to escape from the shadows of secrecy and allow the druids to escape from the prison of the forest?'

'I will,' Arthur assured her.

Releasing all her anxieties and frustrations, Eleri ran across the room. She threw her arms around Arthur, burying her head in his chest. 'Then my sacrifice will be worthwhile,' she sighed.

'There will be no sacrifice,' Arthur said, his eyes fixed on an imaginary point in the middle-distance, his hand caressing Eleri's luxurious auburn hair. 'I will do all that I can to save you.'

'But what can you do?' Eleri said sotto voce.

'I have talked with Morganna. She will speak the truth about Pasgen and in return I must claim her son as my own.'

'You cannot do that!' Horrified, Eleri pulled away from Arthur, her face displaying her revulsion, her eyes revealing her concern. 'I will not let you.'

'I will do what I think is right.'

'But this cannot be right!' Eleri insisted. 'When the child becomes a man your words will lead to conflict.'

'Maybe so,' Arthur agreed, his hand once again reaching out and caressing Eleri's hair. In turn, she took hold of his other hand, entwining her fingers with his. Then, she brought his fingers to her lips and gently kissed them. Looking into her eyes, he sighed: 'I can live with the prospect of conflict, but I cannot live with the prospect of losing you.'

The sound of heavy footsteps echoed in the corridor. Then, the guard opened the door. Arthur and Eleri turned their heads, holding on to each other as Archbishop Dyfrig entered the room.

'Eleri of Ergyng,' the archbishop demanded, 'will you abjure your pagan beliefs before God?'

'I will not!' Eleri declared decisively.

'Then I must invite you to the trial.'

Chapter Twenty

Arthur watched as Archbishop Dyfrig and two guards escorted Eleri to the north-west of the villa and the freshwater pool. He was about to follow them and join the tribal leaders gathered at the pool when Bedwyr and Cai approached from the west.

'We have been talking with traders at the quayside,' Bedwyr said. 'They have some information that might be of interest.'

'What information?' Arthur frowned.

'Led by Illan, Irish currachs have been seen, in great numbers, off the west coast.'

'Sailing towards our shore?'

Slowly, Bedwyr nodded in affirmation: 'That appears to be their intention.'

'Why would they land here?' Arthur mused, his fingers caressing his chin, outlining a layer of dark stubble.

'An invasion?' Cai suggested.

'Unlikely,' Arthur reasoned. 'Before an invasion the Irish would ally with Vortipor. Indeed an alliance with Vortipor would increase their strength and therefore their chance of success.'

'Maybe Vortipor is ignorant of his kindred,' Bedwyr considered, 'and blameless on this occasion.'

'Who will offer support to the Irish?' Arthur asked. 'True, they could attack us without Vortipor's assistance, but why wait until this moment? Why attack us now, when we are blessed with the extra strength of Cadwallon's men, Eleri's men and others, gathered for the Round Table? Why not wait and attack us when we stand as a teulu, alone?'

Arthur cast his gaze towards the west and the coast. The first light of dawn presented a view across the sea to the distant horizon. The sea was calm, the wind was fair and the morning offered the promise of fine sailing. Arthur examined the coastline, but no vessels drifted into view. Yet, he knew from experience that Bedwyr would be sure of his sources and that he spoke the truth; the Irish were out there, somewhere, awaiting their moment, awaiting a signal, preparing to attack. The questions remained: with whom would they ally? When would they attack?

'Also,' Bedwyr said, 'we heard talk that Marc landed along the coast two days before his stated arrival. Therefore, he lied when he spoke of a delay and of the winds being against him.'

Arthur cast his mind back to the first sight of Marc's vessel as that ship sailed into shallow water. He recalled his surprise; he remembered his disquiet, for the lookouts should have seen the ship as soon as the sails appeared on the horizon. He evoked the memory of berating the lookouts and now he realised that he owed them an apology, for Marc had apparently landed at a point further along the coast before making his way to the villa via coastal waters.

'Why would Marc lie?' Arthur deliberated, giving voice to his thoughts.

'On that, you must confront Marc and learn the truth,' Bedwyr said, his tone dark, his glance towards Cai suggesting that he knew the answer and the problems it would create.

'Thank you,' Arthur said. He extended his arms and slapped his companions on their backs. 'You are true friends, loyal allies. You are deserving of my trust.'

With Bedwyr and Cai at his side Arthur walked to the pool. There, he found Ambrosius, his face impassive, as though carved from marble, and Cadwallon, his expression grim yet determined. Vortipor stood with a look of eager anticipation upon his face while Caradog's fingers itched impatiently upon the hilt of his sword, his scowl suggesting that he was ready for a fight.

Before any words could be exchanged Dyfrig appeared at the head of a solemn procession. Clutching his wooden cross firmly in his right hand, he led Eleri towards the pool. The guards had removed Eleri's mantle allowing the freshening breeze to tug at her linen tunic and tangle her long auburn hair. Placing a hand to her face, Eleri brushed her hair from her eyes before glancing at Arthur. Her pleading look compelled him to step forward and challenge Ambrosius:

'This is not justice,' Arthur objected. 'We should secure the truth by other means.'

'The trial will be fair,' Ambrosius intoned, his gaze cast down to the ground. 'Hold your tongue and hold your sword. Place your trust in God and His mercy.'

Unable to contain his frustration, Arthur strode towards Dyfrig. Sensing the possibility of danger, the two guards threatened to intervene. However, after Ambrosius had inclined his head the guards held their ground. The path was now clear and Arthur was free to confront the archbishop:

'Will this please Rome?' Arthur said, his indignant expression demanding an answer. 'Will this please God?'

'It will please Rome to learn the truth,' the archbishop said bluntly. 'Stand aside; allow God to be our judge.'

With his feet planted firmly and his arms folded stubbornly across his chest, Arthur held his ground.

'More words, more delays,' Vortipor complained, his beseeching tone matched by his earnest expression. 'Let our actions speak for us and speak for the truth.'

'I agree,' Cadwallon said, adding his voice to the argument; 'we must delay no longer; we must learn the truth.'

'Place Eleri in the coracle,' Ambrosius commanded. 'Restrain Arthur at sword-point, should he choose to interfere.'

Immediately, Vortipor's hand went to his sword, an action matched by Cadwallon and Caradog.

'There will be no need for swords,' Eleri said. 'Lead me to the coracle and allow me to prove my innocence.'

With her head held high Eleri walked towards the coracle and the pool. Fed by freshwater springs the pool covered an area of some sixty-five acres. Its depth varied, although in certain places one man could stand on the shoulders of another and still not break the surface. The pool was also renowned for its reed beds, which threatened to trap and entangle the unwary. Indeed, many people had taken to the water, never to be seen again.

While one of the guards held Eleri secure in the coracle, the other took hold of a paddle. Skilfully, he eased the craft towards the centre of the pool. Then, Archbishop Dyfrig raised his wooden cross and the guard thrust Eleri head-first into the water. All those gathered beside the pool took a step towards the water's edge. Silently, Arthur counted, up to thirty, but there was no sign of Eleri breaking the surface. Slowly, the number reached sixty and murmurings from the tribal leaders suggested that Eleri had met her fate and that, ironically, the trial had proved her innocence. Arthur was about to abandon the count and abandon all hope of seeing Eleri again when spluttering and gasping she rose to the surface.

After pausing to ensure that Eleri was indeed swimming towards the coracle, Archbishop Dyfrig announced: 'Eleri of Ergyng is guilty of Pasgen's murder. In accordance with our laws, she must burn at the stake. It is, therefore, our duty to collect brushwood for her pyre.'

Chapter Twenty-One

While the guards escorted Eleri back to the villa, Arthur went in search of Marc. Despite entering every room and talking to every person he encountered, Arthur caught no sight of Marc and heard no word of his location. The Lord of Dumnonia had disappeared, as mysteriously as he had arrived in Glywysing.

Marc was nowhere to be seen. However, Arthur did observe Gwenhwyfar as she strolled along the beach. If he could not talk with Marc in person, Arthur reasoned, then maybe he could have words with Gwenhwyfar and seek the truth from her instead.

Arthur walked away from the villa, from the disturbing sight of people wandering around, gathering brushwood for Eleri's pyre. He stepped on to the sand and followed Gwenhwyfar's footsteps as they wandered towards the shoreline.

The ebb tide had left the sand damp and plentiful and so there were many footsteps to follow before Arthur encountered Gwenhwyfar. She was standing at the water's edge, allowing the tide to wash over her feet, a hand placed to her forehead, shielding her emerald-green eyes, as she gazed out to sea.

'It has been a long time,' Arthur said, as he approached Gwenhwyfar. Stubbornly, the capricious lady remained rooted to the spot, a hand still held above her eyes, offering her back to Arthur.

'I am surprised that you remember me,' she said after Arthur had sent a pebble skimming across the sea, its skipping path finally capturing her attention.

'What happened to Medraut, your lover?' Arthur said, bluntly.

'Marc happened to Medraut; I fell in love with Marc.'

'And after Marc?' Arthur enquired.

'Marc is the love of my life,' Gwenhwyfar sighed. She placed a hand to her hair and gave her golden tresses a haughty flick, 'there will be no one after Marc.'

Maybe, Arthur thought, but he held his tongue. Instead, he stooped and scooped up a piece of flotsam from the beach, a length of driftwood. Then, using the driftwood as a stylus, he scratched a shape in the sand.

'You were not at the trial,' he stated.

Gwenhwyfar grimaced, her beautiful face creasing in revulsion: 'I find such trials so distasteful.'

'Neither was Marc.'

'He is above such things,' Gwenhwyfar said, while offering a dismissive wave of her hand.

'Where is Marc?' Arthur asked, his gaze wandering to the shape he was etching in the sand, the hull of a large vessel.

'I do not know; Marc has people to meet, trade and treaties to discuss.'

'The same trade and treaties that delayed his arrival in Glywysing?'

The sea breeze tugged at Gwenhwyfar's shawl revealing her tunic. In turn, the combination of sea breeze and close-fitting tunic exposed the sensual contours of her body. Arthur offered a casual glance at those contours before his gaze settled on Gwenhwyfar's mouth, observing that she was preoccupied, biting her lip.

Gathering her senses, Gwenhwyfar adjusted her shawl, placing it neatly upon her shoulders. Then, she said casually: 'The winds delayed our arrival.'

'Strange,' Arthur continued, his stylus adding a sail to the ship that was taking shape in the sand, 'I thought the winds were in your favour.'

Steadfastly, Gwenhwyfar stared at the sea, paying close attention to the waves as they rolled towards the shore. Her expression was fixed, her mouth set in a thin line. Once again, she adjusted her shawl.

'Marc's boats were seen,' Arthur said, 'two days before his stated arrival in Glywysing.'

For the first time that morning, Gwenhwyfar turned to face Arthur, her angry expression and sharp tone revealing that her querulous nature remained intact.

'Your jealousy towards Marc is misplaced,' Gwenhwyfar said; 'it offers you no favours.'

'I am not jealous of Marc,' Arthur said, truthfully.

Two patches of red burned fiercely high upon Gwenhwyfar's cheekbones, betraying her true feelings. Nevertheless, she offered Arthur a painful smile by way of reply followed by a careless flick of her hair.

'Medraut is jealous of Marc,' Gwenhwyfar said, tetchily.

'I am not Medraut,' Arthur said with a smile, a smile that warmed his dark eyes. Returning to his stylus and the sand, Arthur added a man and a woman to his illustration. Then, apparently satisfied, he stepped back to admire his creation. 'This reminds me of my childhood,' Arthur sighed, 'and the days I walked along this beach with my parents.'

'That is a childish drawing,' Gwenhwyfar said churlishly, 'and I am growing weary of your childish games. I must return to the villa.'

'When did you arrive in Glywysing?' Arthur asked, driving the stylus into the sand and blocking Gwenhwyfar's path.

'The day you saw us step upon the shore.'

'As I mentioned before,' Arthur said patiently, 'you were seen earlier.'

'That is not true,' Gwenhwyfar insisted, her feet betraying her sense of unease as they disturbed the smooth surface of the sand. 'The people who whispered such profanity into your ear must have been mistaken.'

Offended, Arthur shook his head in decisive fashion. 'Your loyalty to Marc is admirable, greater than any loyalty you displayed to me. However,' he continued, 'you can rest assured; Bedwyr and Cai are not mistaken.'

As the waves rolled over her feet, caressing the hem of her gown, Gwenhwyfar realised that she could no longer withhold the truth. With a heavy sigh, she said: 'All right, we arrived some days ago, but for no ill purpose; Marc had trade to attend to.'

'What sort of trade?'

'He did not say.'

'Does Marc yearn to be Pendragon?' Arthur asked.

'No,' Gwenhwyfar insisted; 'Marc says that he has no time for his fellow nobles; it is no enviable task to keep them in order.'

'Did Marc kill Pasgen?'

'For what reason?' Gwenhwyfar scoffed.

'I dare not think,' Arthur admitted. 'Maybe you can suggest a reason.'

'I think that you outstay your welcome,' Gwenhwyfar said, her feet intruding upon Arthur's drawing, her hand pushing the driftwood stylus to the ground.

'I will take my leave,' Arthur conceded, 'but first I will offer you this solemn promise: if your words are a lie then, along with Marc, you will face the consequences.'

Chapter Twenty-Two

Morganna stood on a sandbank and observed as Arthur conversed with Gwenhwyfar. Try as she might she was unable to hear the conversation. However, Gwenhwyfar's gesticulations and Arthur's probing suggested to her that all was not well between them and she concluded that such animosity could only aid her plan.

Leaving the beach, Gwenhwyfar returned to the villa courtyard. Her footsteps took her to within touching distance of her sister, yet she chose to ignore her. With head bowed and eyes cast down to the ground, Gwenhwyfar shuffled towards the sanctuary of her room.

Meanwhile, on the sandbank, Morganna smiled as she realised that Arthur was walking towards her. Without pause for thought, she adjusted her gown, revealing more of her cleavage. The wind tugged at her hair blowing her tresses over her eyes, obscuring her vision and, by the time she had untangled her hair, freeing it from her eyes, she discovered that Arthur was standing before her.

'I am in need of the truth,' Arthur said brusquely.

Raising her right hand, Morganna ran her fingers through her hair, revealing dark, smiling eyes. She paused, her tongue caressing her lips as she savoured the moment. 'If I offer you the truth,' she said, 'will you honour your part of the agreement?'

'Who murdered Pasgen?' Arthur demanded.

Once again, Morganna's hand went to her hair as she fought the entanglement caused by the sea breezes. The wind was rising, yet the sky remained clear; the day offered fair travel for sailors and their cargos.

'Let us discuss this in my room,' Morganna proposed, her eyes sparkling in suggestive fashion.

'That was not a part of the agreement,' Arthur said firmly.

'Then I cannot have you?' Morganna mumbled in a small voice, coyly looking up at him through long, dark eyelashes.

'You cannot.'

'Very well,' she sighed. With a shrug of her shoulders, she continued: 'I will remove such thoughts from my mind.'

Turning her back on the shoreline, Morganna followed her sister's footsteps and the path that led to the villa. True, she felt a sense of disappointment at Arthur's rejection. However, that disappointment was tempered by the realisation that Arthur needed her and his need would fuel her plan.

'You are a man of honour,' Morganna said to Arthur as he joined her on the sandy path, 'you will not break your word?'

'My word will hold true.'

'Then, I will announce to the world that you are the father of my son.'

'If you tell me who murdered Pasgen,' Arthur said, 'then you can make that announcement.'

'Marc murdered Pasgen,' Morganna said dispassionately. 'Marc arranged a meeting in the forest; he argued with Pasgen, then, while Pasgen's back was turned, Marc struck him with the pommel of his sword.'

'You will speak out about this?'

'I will,' Morganna nodded.

Arthur nodded in turn, as though satisfied. Then, he asked: 'Why did Marc kill Pasgen?'

'I have no idea. They were in dispute about something, but the source of that dispute I do not know.'

'And that is the truth?'

'That is the truth,' Morganna insisted.

Morganna waited for Arthur's reaction, for an outburst of emotion, a show of anger. Instead, he turned away, his gaze lost on the horizon, his thoughts hidden, remaining a mystery to her, his true feelings guarded by an impenetrable shield.

While running a hand over her abdomen, Morganna said: 'You should offer a name for our son; do you have a preference?'

'I have none,' Arthur said curtly. Turning to face Morganna, he offered her an intense stare. 'You are condemning your child before he is born. Your actions will ensure that he is brought up to conflict; better to grant him anonymity and peace.'

'Better to allow him to have power and position,' Morganna said harshly, her features losing all sense of their beauty, her anger and frustration on display for all to see. 'I like Amr,' she added decisively. 'We will call him Amr.'

Again, Morganna waited for Arthur's reaction. Instead, he turned his back on her and strode purposefully towards the villa.

Out of frustration, Morganna wanted to cry. Instead, she caressed her abdomen and laughed. Furthermore, she comforted herself with the notion that all men were fools and through love and sex so easy to manipulate.

Chapter Twenty-Three

With Dyfrig at the head of the procession, the tribal leaders - Ambrosius, Caradog, Marc, Vortipor, Cadwallon and Gwenhwyfar - marched towards the brushwood pyre. Servants from the villa had constructed the pyre near a cliff top allowing the wind to capture the lighter elements of kindling and deposit them in the sea. Seabirds circled overhead and, on nearby branches, ravens sat waiting, anticipating their moment.

Two guards led Eleri towards the pyre, guiding her with a length of rope. The guards had tied the rope to Eleri's wrists and the fibres bit into her flesh, drawing blood. At the pyre, the guards paused and Eleri bowed her head. Then, Ambrosius glanced at Archbishop Dyfrig and the churchman made his pronouncement:

'Through God's judgement Eleri of Ergyng is guilty of worshipping druidic gods and of murder. Her body and soul must be cleansed by flame.'

Perturbed, Caradog Strong-arm took a step forward, challenging Ambrosius. With his hirsute features creasing into a questioning frown, he said: 'Are you sure?'

Slowly, Ambrosius nodded and, without any enthusiasm, he confirmed: 'The judgement is just.'

'Wait!' Arthur yelled. With Bedwyr and Cai at his side the dux bellorum strode towards the tribal leaders. Standing beside the pyre, he turned to face Ambrosius. 'The judgement is unjust,' Arthur insisted. 'Marc of Dumnonia killed Pasgen. They arranged a meeting in the forest, where they argued. In anger, Marc struck Pasgen with the pommel of his sword.'

'For what reason?' Ambrosius asked.

'I am not sure,' Arthur admitted. 'However, the Irish and their leader, Illan, are sailing close to our shore and it appears as though they are waiting for someone or something, possibly a signal. They were seen by my men yesterday.'

In unison, the tribal leaders turned to glare at Vortipor. In reply, the Lord of Demetia adopted a defensive posture, shrugging his shoulders and holding his arms out wide.

'I know nothing of Illan and his plans for the Irish,' Vortipor insisted, his voice akin to a teenage whine. 'I am not a branch of their schemes or ambitions.'

Slowly, Ambrosius adjusted his position and, following his lead, the tribal leaders turned to stare at Marc. With a jovial, friendly smile, Marc shook his head and said: 'I have no alliance with the Irish.'

'Then why did you kill Pasgen?' Arthur challenged.

'I did not kill Pasgen and, furthermore, I plead with you, Arthur, that you should desist and not allow our friendship to be destroyed in the furnace of ambition.'

'Our friendship ended with your deception,' Arthur said. Turning to face his companions, he added: 'Bedwyr and Cai learned that your boat arrived on our shore two days before your stated arrival. You lied about your arrival, you lie about the murder.'

'You are mistaken!' Marc insisted. 'The trial by ordeal proved that Eleri is guilty of murder.'

'The pommel of your sword struck Pasgen a fatal blow,' Arthur said, his gaze returning to Marc. 'If you had any honour, you would admit that fact.'

After shaking his head, Marc cast his eyes down to the ground. When he glanced up through his chestnut coloured fringe, those eyes contained a hint of impish mischief, accentuated by the twisted smile that played around his lips.

Stepping forward, Marc placed a hand on Arthur's shoulder. Then, he said: 'I am saddened by your words, Arthur. Does our battle at the River Bassas mean nothing to you?'

'The battle at the River Bassas makes this accusation all the more painful to voice.'

'Then I suggest that you prove your words or hold your tongue.' Withdrawing his hand from

Arthur's shoulder, Marc turned his attention to the tribal leaders. After fixing his gaze upon each and every one of them, he said: 'Arthur cannot prove his claims and he makes them only out of desperation to save Eleri.'

A general murmur of agreement, instigated by Vortipor and given credence by Cadwallon, spread among the tribal leaders. In turn, the leaders looked to Ambrosius, awaiting his decision. Slowly, the Pendragon nodded and the guards escorted Eleri to the waiting pyre.

The guards were about to tie Eleri to the stake when, like a spectral vision appearing through the morning mist, Morganna emerged through the trees. In an uncharacteristically demure voice, she said: 'I can prove Arthur's claims. He speaks the truth. I witnessed the murder; Marc killed my husband.'

Now, the murmur of discontent and the accusing stares alighted on Marc of Dumnonia. In typical, charming fashion, Marc offered a shrug of his shoulders and a disarming smile as his shield.

'Why not speak out before this day?' Ambrosius said to Morganna.

'I would have spoken out but, being a woman, and a lone voice, I was held by fear. With no one to protect and support me, I considered that my words would fall on stony ground.'

Nodding slowly, Ambrosius displayed his understanding. Then, in a firm and decisive voice, he said: 'Release Eleri.'

'This is not just!' Marc protested. Angrily, he drew his sword and waved the weapon at Ambrosius. 'I demand the right to prove my innocence. I will fight with my accusers and trust in God to be my judge.'

'Trial by combat,' Cadwallon mused while arching an eyebrow and stroking his chin. Savouring the idea, he inclined his head in approving fashion.

'Will anyone accept Marc's challenge?' Ambrosius asked, his gaze wandering from Cadwallon to Caradog to Vortipor.

'I will,' Arthur confirmed before anyone could raise their voice or step forward.

'Then let justice be done on this day,' Ambrosius declared. 'Arthur and Marc will fight when the sun reaches its highest point in the sky. God will smile upon the victor and the vanquished will be condemned to hell, along with his sin.'

Chapter Twenty-Four

Arthur stood in the villa courtyard, Caledfwlch held high in his right hand, his shield gripped securely in his left hand, protecting his chest.

Slowly, carefully, Cai moved in a semi-circle, his gaze fixed on Arthur, his sword held firmly in his right hand. Lunging forward, Cai probed for a weakness. However, Arthur was too quick for him and he parried the blow.

From the courtyard fence, Ambrosius watched as Cai swung his sword over Arthur's head, before altering the angle of his attack with a swipe aimed at Arthur's legs. Once again, the dux bellorum was too nimble and he even allowed himself the suggestion of a smile as he evaded the assault.

With a groan of aggression and frustration, Cai offered a muscular thrust, which Arthur deflected via Caledfwlch and a strong right wrist. Grimacing, Cai glared at Arthur with his one good eye, his sword held at arm's length, its tip cutting the breeze as it sought a path to flesh.

Stepping to his left, and then to his right, Cai brought his sword down in an arc, scribed over his left shoulder. Anticipating the blow, Arthur raised his shield and his protector absorbed the might of Cai's belligerence.

Off balance, Cai stumbled, his weight supported by the courtyard fence. Sensing his moment, Arthur thrust Caledfwlch towards Cai's torso, a blow Cai defended with his shield. Nonetheless, Cai was pinned to the fence and forced on to the defensive as Arthur probed and prodded with Caledfwlch, the angle of attack altered with each successive thrust.

Using his shield as a weapon, Arthur struck Cai a firm blow upon his right elbow. The blow weakened Cai's grip on his sword and, with a well-timed strike from Caledfwlch, Arthur removed that sword from Cai's hand.

With only his shield for protection, Cai leaned back against the courtyard fence. Unable to suppress a smile, or stifle his satisfaction, Arthur placed the tip of his sword against Cai's chin.

'Enough!' Ambrosius yelled, his steady tread taking him to the scene of the skirmish, his hand then resting on Arthur's shoulder. 'Save your strength for Marc.'

'That I will do,' Arthur said, sheathing Caledfwlch.

'Well done,' Cai grimaced. 'Another ten victories and we will be equal.'

At that, Arthur laughed. Then, he stooped to gather up Cai's sword before offering the weapon to his friend.

'We fight amongst ourselves, we seek division rather than union and we remain blind to the Saxon threat,' Ambrosius said as Cai made his way towards a barrel of water. Cai splashed some of the water over his hair and face. Then, he strode purposefully towards Bedwyr and his elevated position, overlooking the coast.

'The Saxons will be dealt with,' Arthur said, 'as soon as I have dealt with Marc.'

'And what of Illan and his Irish marauders?'

'Bedwyr and Cai will keep a good watch along the coast. If Illan and the Irish land, we will be the first to know.'

Ambrosius' gaze wandered towards the coast. Slowly, he nodded, for he knew that Bedwyr and Cai were meticulous about their tasks and that they would provide fair warning, should the Irish disembark and set foot upon the shores of Glywysing. Nevertheless, a doubt remained, a doubt that found its voice when Ambrosius turned to face Arthur.

'I hope that you are right in every respect,' Ambrosius said. 'Furthermore, I hope that your defence of Eleri will not offend God.'

'God should not be offended by time-honoured beliefs or time out of mind beliefs. Indeed, we can demonstrate just how strong the Christian Church is through tolerance of such beliefs. A country cannot be at peace with itself unless it embraces all manner of beliefs, including the beliefs of all its people. This is the meaning of unity; celebrating diversity, not suffering under a forced dictum, a dictum that states that all must worship as the leaders do. We must unite, but each tribe, each person, must be free to worship the god of their choice.'

'And what of Rome?' Ambrosius asked, his voice strained, burdened by the struggle.

'Rome will remain strong. Nevertheless, we must face our reality. To defeat the Saxons, we must have a stronger sense of unity; we must all stand together, or we will fall. And I have come to realise that we can only find that unity through recognising our diversity, our individual strengths and beliefs.'

'But, if not Rome,' Ambrosius persisted, 'then what will bind us together?'

Smiling, Arthur bent his back and scooped up a handful of soil. With the soil held secure in the palm of his hand, he presented it to Ambrosius. 'This land will bind us together, our love of this land and the recognition of our shared traditions. And those traditions have their roots in time-honoured beliefs, beliefs held long before the days of Rome.'

Simultaneously, Ambrosius scowled and nodded, demonstrating a painful understanding of the situation. With the scowl still fixed upon his face, he said: 'I fought against Vortigern because he stood against Rome; was I wrong to do so?'

'You were right to do so,' Arthur said, 'because Vortigern stole our lands and gave those lands to the Saxons. He was a tyrant. You have been a Pendragon.'

In response, Ambrosius allowed himself a watery smile. He acknowledged Arthur's words by placing a hand upon his shoulder. Then, Eleri and Caradog captured his attention as they entered the courtyard.

'Judge me by my sword,' Arthur said. 'If I am victorious against Marc, that victory will show that God still walks at my side.'

'I will do that,' Ambrosius said firmly, 'I will allow God to be my judge.'

'Enough chatter,' Caradog said; 'you carry on like washerwomen. Arthur should rest his sword arm and his tongue. And he must show no mercy when he confronts Marc.'

Standing before Arthur, Eleri held out her right hand. Unfurling her fingers, she revealed a gold chain and a gold pendant depicting the symbol of Mabon, a solar wheel containing four spokes. 'A talisman,' she explained, 'this will ensure your success, for today and for evermore.'

Inclining his head, Arthur allowed Eleri to place the talisman around his neck. Then, she ran the back of her hand over the bristles on his cheek before adding a gentle kiss.

'Are you ready?' Ambrosius asked, his gaze fixed on the sun as the golden orb rose to its highest point in the sky.

'I am ready,' Arthur confirmed.

'Then let us delay no longer,' Ambrosius said; 'let battle commence and let justice be done.'

Chapter Twenty-Five

Arthur stood beside the pyre, flexing his fingers over the hilt of Caledfwlch. With unblinking eyes, he stared at the villa as he waited for Marc. Servants had staked and roped a large area of ground, thirty paces by thirty paces, in preparation for the trial by combat. Should either man break the boundary designated by the rope then that man would lose the contest.

Ambrosius stood beside the rope along with Caradog, Vortipor, Dyfrig, Morganna and Eleri. Everyone gazed at the villa, awaiting Marc's arrival. Indeed, so engrossed were the tribal leaders that no one acknowledged Bedwyr as he abandoned his observation post and strode to Arthur's side.

'Any sign of the Irish currachs?' Arthur asked, his eyes still focused on the villa.

'The sea is devoid of vessels,' Bedwyr replied. 'The waters are calm and as empty as a drunkard's beaker.'

Arthur responded by nodding slowly. Then, his eyes narrowed as he caught sight of Cadwallon, emerging from the villa.

'Your sword will not cleave flesh today,' Cadwallon announced as he approached Arthur.

'Marc is not at the villa. Gwenhwyfar too has disappeared.'

Arthur's eyes settled on Bedwyr before returning to the villa and Bedwyr knew instantly that Arthur's gaze was a signal for him to investigate.

'Maybe Marc feared your sword and took to his boat?' Caradog suggested as Bedwyr made his way towards the villa. 'Maybe someone would like to take Marc's place, someone whose tongue has been well exercised in accusing Eleri?'

Prompted by Caradog, heads turned and eyes glared at Vortipor.

'I have no wish to take Marc's place,' Vortipor said defensively, his hands raised to his shoulders, his open palms offered to the tribal leaders as though indicating that he had nothing to hide. 'Clearly, I was wrong. Marc's absence proves his guilt; he murdered Pasgen. Therefore, Eleri is innocent. I ask Arthur for his forgiveness.'

'Don't ask me,' Arthur said brusquely, 'ask the noble lady.'

Reluctantly, Vortipor turned and bowed before Eleri, his back bending slowly and grudgingly, as though he were an octogenarian and not a young man who had recent memory of his youth. 'Eleri of Ergyng,' Vortipor said, his head turned, his eyes avoiding direct contact, 'with all humility, I ask for your forgiveness.'

'Granted,' Eleri replied with no hint of inflection in her voice.

As Vortipor straightened his back and took his place beside the tribal leaders, Bedwyr returned from the villa. With nimble feet making haste over the ground, he approached Arthur and said: 'Cadwallon speaks the truth. What is more, it appears as though Marc did not flee alone; Cerdic is no longer in his prison.'

Arthur paused, his fingers caressing the dark stubble upon his chin. After a thoughtful interlude, he reasoned: 'So, it would appear that Marc and Cerdic are in league, hence the murder. Pasgen discovered their alliance, maybe when he talked with Cerdic. Later, he confronted Marc only to feel the weight of Marc's sword. If I am right, then Marc has allied himself with the Saxons.'

'If you are right,' Ambrosius said, 'then Marc must have had in mind another night of the long knives. Marc would have informed the Saxons of our plans and then provided access to our camp. The Saxons would have killed all the tribal leaders gathered here at this Round Table.'

Bowing their heads, the tribal leaders lapsed into silence as they considered the gravity of Ambrosius' words. The Saxons had gained a secure foothold in their country thanks to the night of the long knives; another such slaughter would see the Saxons claim the remainder of the island.

'This explains Cerdic's presence in our region,' Arthur added. 'Furthermore, the safe harbour provided by Marc would make the voyage easier for the Saxon keels, for those keels could arrive in force with no fear of impediment.'

'Arthur is right,' Caradog said. 'Therefore, we cannot sit back and wait for the Saxons to attack; we must pursue Marc and Cerdic.'

'There will be a battle,' Bedwyr said.

'We will need a leader,' Caradog smiled.

Unsheathing his sword, Caradog held the weapon by its blade, offering the hilt to Ambrosius, a deed that the tribal leaders repeated to a man. However, instead of accepting the swords, Ambrosius bowed his head and said:

'I am too old to lead you in battle. Nevertheless, for one last time, I will allow my wisdom to guide you as Pendragon. Arthur has been vindicated. God has spoken. Arthur is my dux bellorum and he will lead you in battle.'

'Does anyone object?' Eleri asked, her resolute tone and her determined expression defying words of opposition.

'Arthur has my sword,' Caradog stated proudly, his chest swelling as he uttered his words.

'My sword belongs to Arthur,' Vortipor echoed, although his tone lacked any great enthusiasm or warmth.

'I will recognise Arthur as our dux bellorum,' Cadwallon confirmed. 'However, I still hold a claim to the title of Pendragon. And I will make good that claim when I have defeated the Saxons.'

'First, we must find the Saxons,' Bedwyr said, his gaze wandering from the tribal leaders to the burly figure of Cai. His friend had abandoned the observation post and now he stood beside Arthur, his arm extended as he pointed towards the coastline.

'Look no further,' Cai said, 'for that is not a forest moving across the water; that is a mass of Saxon keels.'

Chapter Twenty-Six

Standing on the ramparts at Badon the tribal leaders watched as the Saxon keels made their way up the river towards the unguarded villa. Arthur had ordered a retreat to the hill fort at Badon and, along with the tribal leaders and their war bands, he waited for the Saxons to land.

'We should have held our ground,' Cadwallon complained, his feet pacing restlessly on the ramparts, 'and confronted the Saxons when they set foot upon our shore.'

'And invite a slaughter?' Arthur smiled. 'The Saxons arrive in force; in terms of fighting men we are outnumbered three to one. Better to retreat and seek the safety of Badon. From here we can fight the Saxons on our own terms.'

Disgruntled, Cadwallon shrugged his lean shoulders. Then he walked to the northern part of the ramparts to join his teulu who had been charged with defending that section of the wall.

Arthur had little time to reflect upon Cadwallon's complaint, for soon he was joined by a belligerent Cai and a thoughtful Bedwyr.

'The walls are secure and well manned?' Arthur enquired.

'Indeed, they are,' Cai replied.

'The archers are ready?' Arthur asked.

'Awaiting your signal,' Bedwyr assured him.

'And what of the gateway?' Arthur frowned. 'Our weakest point is well defended?'

'I have placed our best men there,' Cai said. 'The Saxons would have a better chance of walking through the fires of hell than of walking through our gateway.'

'Then we are ready,' Arthur smiled. 'Rejoin your men,' he instructed. 'Await my signal.'

Without further ado, Bedwyr and Cai complied with Arthur's command and, as they walked away, the dux bellorum was joined by Archbishop Dyfrig.

'What should I do?' Dyfrig asked, his fingers tapping his wooden cross in agitated fashion.

'Escort the women and children to the monastery at Mynydd-y-Gaer,' Arthur said. 'Then pray to God for our success.'

As the afternoon sunlight faded, the Saxons set foot upon Arthur's land and he watched as wave upon wave of warriors marched towards Badon. Occasionally, a shaft of sunlight would reflect upon a row of spears or a line of axes or glint off the bosses of the advancing shield wall. The daylight was rapidly diminishing. However, Arthur judged that the Saxons would reach Badon before dusk.

The early evening chill compelled Arthur to adjust his cloak, pulling the garment tightly around his shoulders. Nevertheless, true warmth only touched his bones when he caught sight of Eleri.

'We will be victorious,' the Lady of Ergyng said while standing at Arthur's side.

'I thank you for your confidence, but how can you be so sure?'

'I am sure because you are the man who leads us. And,' she added with a smile, 'because I prayed to the ancestors.'

A number of Saxons had remained at the coast to guard their keels. Now, some of them lit the pyre intended for Eleri and, hell-bent on destruction, they spread that flame to the villa courtyard and on to the villa itself.

As the flames burned brightly against the darkening sky, Ambrosius and Caradog joined Arthur on the ramparts. In silence, the three men gazed at the destruction, their expressions grim, their stares hardening with determination, while a degree of anger scorched their souls.

'The villa is ablaze,' Ambrosius said mournfully.

'Buildings can be rebuilt,' Caradog said, a shrug of his shoulders adding to his philosophical reply.

With the sound of the Saxon war chants growing ever louder, Arthur made a final inspection of his defences. On the northern wall, Cadwallon, Vortipor and their war bands stood guard, ready to repel the invaders. On the southern wall, Eleri and the archers of Ergyng augmented Caradog and the men of Gwent. Meanwhile, Cai, accompanied by a number of the teulu, stood proud above the main gate, while the remainder of his men waited in reserve. Satisfied, Arthur returned to the ramparts. He took his position above the main gate just as the Saxons were breaking into a run and rushing towards Badon.

As the Saxon drums beat a steady, menacing rhythm and their flags flew in the evening breeze, the anticipated volley of spears came hurtling towards the defenders at Badon.

'Keep your heads down and your shields held high!' Arthur commanded as a spear splintered the top right-hand corner of his shield before landing safely at his feet.

Arthur knew that the Saxons were limited to three spears per warrior and so, even though this rain of metal and wood carried with it a lethal threat, this phase of the storm would soon pass.

To his relief, Arthur was accurate in his judgement and although the spears brought a great deal of destruction and many good men were lost, the defences at Badon held secure leaving the Saxons with no option other than to attack with axes and swords.

The Saxons directed the first wave of their attack at the gatehouse. Using their shields for protection, they endeavoured to batter their way into the hill fort. While the shield bearers sought to deflect the volleys of arrows and stones, the warriors pounded the gatehouse door with a carved tree trunk. The gatehouse shook with each blow, the structure trembling beneath Arthur's feet. However, led by Cai, the teulu had constructed firm defences using upturned carts and stakes of wood and iron bars to support the door. Despite the battering, the gatehouse held secure and soon the Saxon threat diminished as the rapidity and accuracy of Bedwyr's archers took its toll.

To the north of the gatehouse, the Saxons attempted to place ladders against the wall and climb to the level of the parapet. Sheer weight of numbers ensured that some of the Saxons reached the top of the wall, only to meet the fury of Cadwallon's teulu and Vortipor's warriors.

The same story was repeated on the southern wall where Saxon aggression was countered by fierce resistance from Eleri and her archers and from Caradog and his men of Gwent.

As the bodies amassed in front of the defensive wall, Arthur judged that the Britons were winning the battle. Nevertheless, a glance to the north told him that the Saxons were making progress in their attempt to burrow under the defences. Furthermore, their efforts threatened to weaken the wall and create a fatal fissure.

'Archers!' Arthur ordered and Bedwyr instructed his men to loosen their arrows at the warriors undermining the wall.

The moon was rising in the sky and still Badon held secure. Soon, Arthur reasoned, the Saxons would have to alter their tactics or call off their attack. Perspiring profusely, Arthur wiped a measure of blood from his face, blood from his own wounds and blood from his companions. Arthur judged that the grazes, caused by the Saxon axes, spears and swords, were insignificant. However, the cries and the groans from the men around him indicated that they had not been so fortunate.

A blast on a horn signalled to the Saxons that they should retreat and those left standing faded into the darkness, a volley of arrows following in their wake. Arthur considered that the Saxons had lost many men and yet they still outnumbered the defenders by a considerable margin.

Turning back to gaze at Badon, and with some relief, Arthur noted that Morganna was organising the care of the wounded. One-by-one, members of her teulu carried or escorted the injured to roundhouses at the centre of the encampment. Those less fortunate would have to be buried by torchlight and that thought strengthened Arthur's resolve: victory would be obtained; from this day on people of all tongues, all tribes, all beliefs would remember the sacrifice and the glory of Badon.

Led by Ambrosius, the tribal leaders approached Arthur. By great fortune and even greater skill, all managed to escape serious injury. To a man, they fought bravely in the battle and to a man, they displayed courage and fortitude.

'Victory is ours,' Vortipor declared wildly, shaking his fist in the air with adrenalin-fuelled passion, the wide-eyed smile on his face and the livid gash on his cheek revealing the emotions and the tribulations of battle.

'Victory is ours when the last Saxon has fallen,' Arthur said. 'For now, many remain standing and they will return. So take your men, my lord Vortipor, repair the defences and make secure the northern wall.'

With a weary shrug of his shoulders, Vortipor acknowledged Arthur's command. Then, he returned to the northern wall and the damage wreaked by the Saxons.

As Vortipor rejoined his teulu, Arthur glanced at Cai, suggesting that he should oversee the repairs. Without hesitation, Cai made his way to the northern wall leaving Arthur to reflect upon the fate of the Saxon chieftains.

'Did anyone catch sight of Marc?' Arthur questioned, his gaze returning to the tribal leaders.

Slowly, and in unison, all shook their heads.

'And what of Aelle and Cerdic?' Arthur continued. 'Did anyone catch sight of them?'

'Typically they wait at the rear,' Caradog said. 'Brave men that they are, they cower behind bushes while their warriors face the might of our swords.'

'Then soon we must set fire to those bushes,' Arthur said. 'We must bring Marc, Cerdic and Aelle to battle and put an end to this war.'

Chapter Twenty-Seven

Night drifted inexorably towards dawn and, with trusted men on guard, Arthur managed a period of fitful sleep. After taking his place on the ramparts above the main gate, Arthur cast an eye over the bloodied landscape and considered what the Saxons would do next. The obvious tactic would be to resume the attack on the weakened northern wall while diverting the defenders with an assault on the gatehouse or southern wall. To Arthur's mind, this approach would eventually lead to success and, therefore, he would have to prepare his men and surprise the Saxons with a strategy that was both measured and audacious.

As Arthur considered his options, Cadwallon approached, the scars of battle still evident upon his arms and face, a crooked smile revealing that a Saxon axe had bloodied his lip and removed his front teeth.

'You did well, Arthur,' Cadwallon said, lisping through the wound. 'When I am Pendragon I will be pleased if you will serve me as dux bellorum.'

Before Arthur could reply, Cadwallon offered another battered smile. Then, he made his way along the ramparts, issuing orders to his men.

The light morning mist evaporated with the dawn and the men of Badon watched and waited, listening for the beat of the Saxon war drums, searching for a glimpse of the Saxon axes and swords. In the bay, Irish currachs drifted into view and it was clear that Illan and his men were about to add strength to the Saxon forces.

Then, taking everyone at Badon by surprise, a lone Saxon approached the hill fort, a white flag fluttering on a broken spear shaft. Ceremoniously, he hurled his axe into the ground before looking up at the gatehouse.

'What game do they play now?' Vortipor frowned, his anxious gaze following the Saxon, his right hand raised, ready to instruct his men.

'Tell your men to curb their aggression,' Arthur said. 'This man comes in peace; we will listen to his words.'

After planting the white flag in the ground, the Saxon stood in front of the gatehouse. Gazing up at the tribal leaders, his eyes searched for Arthur. Eventually, the Saxon located the noble warrior and, in a firm, steady voice, he said: 'Our leaders wish to talk peace.'

'This is a trap,' Vortipor said, his right hand drawing his sword from its scabbard. However, before Vortipor could brandish his sword in anger,

Cai placed a hand upon its hilt, driving the weapon back into its casing.

'We will meet with your leaders,' Arthur told the Saxon, 'three men, unaided, on open ground, by the great oak tree.'

The Saxon turned and located the tall oak tree standing proud and alone in an adjacent meadow. Slowly, he nodded. Then, he said: 'I will notify Aelle.'

As the Saxon returned to his kinsmen, Arthur turned to face the tribal leaders. 'Will anyone join me?' he asked.

'I will,' Cadwallon said.

'I will ride at your side,' Caradog echoed.

Cai and Bedwyr brought the horses to the gatehouse and a path was cleared allowing access to the main gate. Arthur mounted Llamrei. Of course, he could easily walk to the great oak tree. However, the horses provided a rapid means of escape should the Saxons consider betrayal. Furthermore, sitting astride a horse offered the advantage of looking down at your opponent.

Arthur, Cadwallon and Caradog guided their horses to the great oak tree. As they waited under the branches Marc, Cerdic and Aelle approached, the latter wearing a warrior's mask. The mask consisted of decorative bronze panels, covering the crown of Aelle's head, his ears and his cheekbones while oval apertures allowed a glimpse of his bloodshot eyes. Moreover, eyebrows and a moustache had been fashioned on to the mask suggesting to the onlooker that the bronze was organic and alive.

Arthur glared at Marc and Cerdic, the traitors, and he could feel nothing but contempt for them. He stared into Aelle's eyes and thought of his parents and the way they had suffered at the end of Aelle's axe. Arthur considered that Aelle was unaware of his actions all those years ago, of the fact that he had killed Arthur's parents, for he had been a youth then and he had killed so many Britons since that fateful day.

'Are your looks so repulsive that you need to hide your face from us?' Arthur said, his gaze fixed on the bloodshot eyes of Aelle.

'We wish to talk with you,' Aelle said, his right hand removing the mask, revealing a face scarred by battle, a forehead creased with a frown and a jawline as firm as bedrock. 'We come in peace,' Aelle continued, 'and we seek peace, everlasting.'

'Leave our land,' Arthur said, 'and peace will prevail.'

Throwing his head back, Aelle laughed, a light sound, which surprised Arthur given Aelle's ox-like build and the power he exuded.

'We cannot do that,' Aelle said. 'Our people flourish and our numbers increase. Kin join us from our old homeland; we need more land.'

'Then take to your boats,' Arthur said, 'and sail across the sea.'

'We are here!' Aelle said with anger invading his voice. 'We have planted roots here. When we sail, it will be to explore the flow of your rivers.' Pausing, he offered a cold-blooded smile. 'You do not want war, we do not want war, so let us find a path to peace.'

'And where might this path begin?' Arthur said calmly.

'With the granting of land; we demand the rights to the land you call Ergyng and the land you call Gwent.'

'Your demands are small,' Arthur grinned, amused and angered by Aelle's impudence.

'We also demand the rights to the land you call Glywysing.'

Apparently annoyed by Aelle's remark, Llamrei snorted and took a step towards the Saxon leader. As Arthur brought the horse under control he scoffed, then added: 'And where would our people go?'

'Decide amongst yourselves,' Aelle laughed. 'Fight amongst yourselves. You people are good at fighting amongst yourselves.'

Arthur glanced at Cadwallon and Caradog and it was clear from their dogged expressions that they shared Arthur's opposition to Aelle's plan. Shaking his head in resolute fashion, Arthur said: 'We cannot agree to your demands.'

'That is a shame,' Aelle smiled. 'I will have to return to my people and tell them to sharpen their axes. We will both lose many good men. But I will be victorious. And when my victory has been achieved then I will give thanks to my friends from across the water.'

Turning towards the coast, Aelle pointed to Illan and the Irish currachs. Now, the currachs were in position, awaiting a signal, anticipating the moment when they would invade Badon and lay waste to the land.

'I have promised my Irish friends the rights to the land you call Demetia,' Aelle smiled. 'Agree to my terms,' he demanded, 'or face slaughter.'

'Slaughter?' Arthur said. 'If good men should fall then they will fall upon you and all the Saxon leaders.'

'So the battle must continue?' Aelle frowned.

'The battle must continue,' Arthur affirmed, 'to the very end.'

Chapter Twenty-Eight

Before the sun could reach its highest point in the sky, the Saxons returned to Badon. They hurled flaming torches of brushwood, creating numerous fires within the hill fort, and the billowing smoke from those fires brought tears to the eyes of the defenders.

As Arthur had anticipated, the Saxons attacked the southern wall, though the fortification was well defended by Caradog's teulu and by Eleri's archers. However, the attack against the southern wall was little more than a ploy, a manoeuvre designed to occupy the defenders while the main assault continued against the northern wall. The Saxons probed and exploited the weakness in the northern wall, claiming the lives of many brave men, reducing the strength of Cadwallon's teulu and Vortipor's war band. Men from Arthur's teulu supplemented the courageous defence ensuring that Saxon blood flowed over wood and stone and grass.

Using the flames from within Badon, Bedwyr and his archers set fire to their arrows and eventually this flaming terror offered some respite as the Saxons were forced to retreat. Nevertheless,

Arthur realised that the northern wall had been breached beyond reasonable defence and that the Saxons would force their way into Badon by nightfall.

With smoke filling the air and with mist settling on the ground, the tribal leaders gathered at the battle-scarred gatehouse.

'We can no longer hold the northern wall,' Cadwallon said, a gash upon his left shoulder and a wound upon his thigh adding to his facial injuries. 'I suggest that we retreat and construct our defences within Badon.'

Arthur paused. He gazed at Cadwallon, acknowledging his skill and his strength and his courage. Then, with a smile, he dismissed Cadwallon's remarks and turned to Cai. 'Remember Guinnion?' Arthur asked.

Cai nodded and grinned broadly: 'I do; that battle saw a vast slaughter of Saxon axemen. Guinnion was our greatest day.'

'We will replicate that battle,' Arthur said.

'How?' Cadwallon insisted. 'By what means?'

'We will leave Badon,' Arthur said calmly, 'and sacrifice the high ground.'

'And give up our advantage?' Cadwallon frowned.

'Trust me,' Arthur said. 'We surprised the Saxons at Guinnion and achieved a great victory;

we will surprise the Saxons at Badon and reward our people with success.'

Turning to Ambrosius with a beseeching look in his eyes, Vortipor pleaded: 'This is madness; if we leave Badon we will be routed.'

'Arthur is our dux bellorum,' Ambrosius said firmly, his marble jaw set at a determined angle, the familiar flinty look evident in his eyes. 'We follow Arthur; we offer him our trust and, in return, he will offer us victory.'

Without further ado, Arthur turned to his trusted companions, Bedwyr and Cai: 'At the sound of the battle horn enter the fields and light the Beltane fires,' he instructed, 'then assemble the teulu. Caradog, Morganna, Eleri: gather together all the supplies, including all the food. Prepare to abandon Badon.'

Rapidly, the tribal leaders dispersed, allowing Cadwallon an opportunity to approach Arthur. 'Should your plan fail,' Cadwallon warned, sotto voce, 'you will not feel the edge of a Saxon axe; you will feel the sharpness of my blade.'

As the sun began its descent into the western sky, Arthur summoned a member of his teulu. 'Sound the battle horn,' Arthur commanded, and then he watched as Bedwyr and Cai set the fields aflame, the crack of kindling spitting fire into the sky as the dense clouds of smoke blended with the hilltop mist filling the air with its acrid odour.

Under the cover of the smoke cloud, the supplies were gathered and moved to safety, beyond the brow of a tree-lined hill, to the west of Badon. Livestock, horses and people also gathered there and from their sheltered position, they watched as the Saxons charged towards Badon.

Arthur wondered at the Saxons' surprise as they swung their axes against thin air, he considered their reaction as they discovered that no one was there. Even in the midst of the struggle, Arthur was moved to smile.

'The Saxons have captured Badon,' Vortipor stated, his face a mask of sullen despair. 'Meanwhile, we are vulnerable upon this undefended mound.'

'The Saxons have cast themselves adrift from their ships and supplies,' Arthur said. 'Their chain has been broken. I suggest that you stop complaining and ride with haste to the coast; take your men and destroy their ships and supplies.'

Arthur judged that determined men on fast horses would eat up the ground and arrive at the coast before the Saxons had completed their destruction of Badon. It was his fervent hope that the Saxon keels would be set aflame before Aelle ordered a search of the wider landscape.

The afternoon drifted towards evening and Arthur spied Saxon warriors emerging from the gatehouse. A battle amongst the trees was not what Arthur desired. It was vital that Vortipor captured Aelle's attention and drew him and his warriors out on to open ground.

'Your plan has failed,' Cadwallon said bitterly, 'soon the Saxons will discover where we are hiding.'

'My plan will succeed,' Arthur said. 'Trust me, have faith in a fellow Briton.'

'You put your faith in Vortipor,' Cadwallon scoffed. 'I would sooner put my faith in the Devil.'

'Then let Satan be your friend,' Caradog ventured with a smile, his right arm outstretched, his forefinger pointing to a wisp of smoke as it drifted out to sea.

The light, hazy smoke blackened and became dense as the flames embraced the Saxon keels. In consternation, the Saxons emerged from Badon and, led by Aelle, they rushed down the hillside.

'Sound the battle horn,' Arthur said. 'Mount your horses. Scatter the Saxons amongst the fields, but leave Aelle to me.'

At the sound of the battle horn, Cai and his horsemen emerged through the smoke and galloped down the hillside. Now the Britons could rely on their strength; they could fight over open ground on horseback.

'Are you prepared for the fight?' Arthur said, his gaze fixed on Cadwallon.

'I will leave not one Saxon standing,' Cadwallon pledged, before mounting his horse and entering the fray.

Scattered and unable to form their fearsome shield wall, the Saxons fought as individuals on open ground. Their shields and their axes offered a measure of defence and aggression, though they were no match for the teulu and the relentless horsemen. Swords cut through flesh more frequently than axes cleaved through bone and it soon became apparent that the Battle of Badon was turning into a rout.

From their position on sheltered high ground, Bedwyr and his archers purged the Saxon stragglers as, in desperation, they tried to escape the carnage of the battlefield. Meanwhile, guided by Arthur, Llamrei charged over the hillside, the horse careering into Saxons and scattering them like straw. With the momentum offered by the speeding horse, Arthur swung Caledfwlch through wood and metal, through bone and sinew, spilling blood and severing limbs, littering the battlefield with Saxon corpses.

Glancing to his left, Arthur noticed that a Saxon warrior had unseated Cadwallon and that the Lord of Gwynedd was helpless, prone on the ground. The Saxon hoisted his axe and was about to administer a fateful blow when Arthur roused Llamrei. He raised Caledfwlch, charged forward and swung the mighty blade, removing the warrior's arm at the shoulder. An arc of Saxon blood sprayed into the air as the warrior fell on to the ground.

Without pause for breath, Arthur galloped down the hillside in search of Aelle. However, there was no sign of the man or his metal mask amongst the dead bodies and the severed limbs. After a moment of reflection, Arthur encouraged Llamrei to gallop towards Badon, for reason suggested that he would find Aelle there. The horse was about to lengthen his stride when a figure appeared through the mist and the smoke. Bloodied from battle and ragged from the ravages of the sword, Cerdic stood before Arthur, his axe poised, his expression grim.

'The battle is lost,' Arthur said, his voice loud and clear, rising above the cacophony of war noise. 'Save yourself; surrender.'

'You should have killed me when you had the chance,' Cerdic scowled.

With his axe swinging wildly, Cerdic rushed towards Llamrei though, bravely, with nostrils flared the horse stood his ground. Awaiting the moment, Arthur swayed to his left, allowing the axe to cleave thin air. Then, he turned and raised Caledfwlch high above his shoulder before swinging the sword down on to Cerdic's unprotected head.

Another Saxon had fallen and, glancing around the battlefield, Arthur noted that Cerdic was one of a thousand. Yet, there was no sign of Aelle. Encouraging Llamrei, Arthur galloped up the hill and entered Badon.

The fires were still raging and the smoke compelled Llamrei to snort in protest. Sweat foamed on the horse's chest. Nevertheless, Arthur guided Llamrei through the devastation, to the heart of Badon and his roundhouse.

Dismounting and leaving Llamrei at the doorway, Arthur entered the roundhouse. Amongst the burning embers, he found Aelle, his face hidden by his mask, his axe resting against Morganna's neck. Morganna's eyes were wide in fear, while her forehead and her clothing were stained with sweat.

'This act offers you no honour,' Arthur said. 'Free the woman and take your place on the battlefield.'

'I will kill her,' Aelle threatened, 'unless you offer me safe passage to my homeland.'

'And from there,' Arthur countered, 'you will gather your warriors and then we will do battle all over again. No,' he insisted. 'Our dispute ends here, today, at Badon.'

'Arthur!' Morganna cried desperately, only for Aelle to secure her silence by placing his axe to her lips.

As Morganna stared at Arthur through pleading eyes, a thought troubled him: should Aelle kill Morganna then the act would release Arthur from the devil's deal of claiming Morganna's child as his own. Yet, he could not stand by and see the woman and child murdered. His conscience demanded that he should confront Aelle and seek justice through his sword.

'The woman is with child,' Arthur reasoned. 'Free her and pit your axe against my sword. Allow the victor to claim the day.'

Arthur gazed into Aelle's eyes. However, they were glazed and, along with his mask, they hid all emotion. A hand tightening around Morganna's wrist and the axe placed against her neck told Arthur that Aelle remained on the defensive, that he was reluctant to surrender his hostage.

'Very well,' Arthur said, 'we will play this game your way. We will allow the chroniclers to record that Aelle hid behind a woman's gown while his warriors died gloriously upon the battlefield.'

With a growl of anger and frustration, Aelle thrust Morganna to the ground. She fell, coughing and sobbing, on to her knees.

'Run!' Arthur shouted and Morganna scrambled to her feet. She raced to the door, where she paused, glancing over her shoulder.

With Morganna looking on, Arthur strode towards Aelle. In his right hand, he carried Caledfwlch while his left hand caressed the gold pendant depicting the symbol of Mabon, the talisman presented by Eleri.

Holding his axe in both hands, Aelle circled Arthur as a predator circles his prey. In Arthur's right hand, Caledfwlch shone like a numinous wand, its aura of blue glowing through the smoke. Aelle glanced at the sword; weary from battle he knew that one blow would decide the contest; he knew that he had one chance to remove Arthur's head. And so the circling continued until an overwhelming sense of trepidation compelled Morganna to cry out; falling on to her knees, she placed her head in her hands and emitted a long, beseeching wail.

Fleetingly, Arthur glanced at Morganna. Sensing his moment, Aelle raised his axe and prepared to strike. With a savage and bloodthirsty roar, he swung his axe at Arthur's head. Instinct, and years of experience, told Arthur to move his head to his left and the axe cleaved thin air. The vigour and momentum of Aelle's action sent him stumbling towards the door, where he fell on to his knees, his axe biting into the dirt of the roundhouse floor.

Without hesitation, Arthur turned and swung Caledfwlch at Aelle's head, the blow removing Aelle's helmet, the impact sending the mask spinning across the floor. Scrambling to his feet, Aelle reached into his belt and withdrew his sax, a large dagger. With the dagger poised in his hand, he rushed towards Arthur only to encounter the tip of Arthur's sword.

'For my father,' Arthur said as Caledfwlch bit deep into sinew. 'For my mother,' he added as the sword found its way through flesh.

With a cry of anguish, Aelle fell on to the ground, clutching his chest. With his eyes wide open, he registered a glimmer of understanding before a convulsive shudder removed the last of his breath.

Reaching for the talisman, Arthur placed the pendant to his lips. Then, he offered his hand to Morganna and escorted her out of the roundhouse.

Chapter Twenty-Nine

With a pensive Morganna at his side, Arthur walked through the debris of Badon. It would take time to rebuild the structures within the hill fort and the lives of its occupants. However, Arthur reflected, at least those lives could contemplate acts of peace and be free from the fear of war.

'You saved my life,' Morganna whispered, her voice somehow distant, her eyes still wide and wild, her face displaying the trauma of battle. 'I should offer you my gratitude.'

'Allow your child to live in peace,' Arthur said. 'Remove the pledge you forced me to make.'

As though in a daze, Morganna walked on in silence. Then, abruptly, she stopped. With her fingers caressing her abdomen and her eyes cast down to the ground, she said: 'I cannot do that. My child must grow up with the belief that he will become Pendragon.'

'That is a false belief,' Arthur said.

Glancing up, Morganna met Arthur's gaze. In that instant some of the fire returned to Morganna's eyes, some of her passion, belief and determination.

'You are wrong,' Morganna said. 'When my son is a man he will prove himself worthy; the Britons will acknowledge him as their leader.'

'If that is the will of the people,' Arthur said. 'However, if the people oppose such imposition then I pray that my strength will prevail and, if need be, I will raise a teulu against him.'

Turning away, Morganna flinched, her pained expression suggesting that Arthur had struck her. She took a deep breath and then, regaining her composure, she caressed her womb. With the suggestion of a smile playing around her lips, she said: 'You must honour your pledge. Even so, as a show of gratitude I will hold back the announcement of my son's lineage until the day he is born.'

Then, with her back proud and straight and her head held high, Morganna walked away from Arthur. She disappeared into the mist and gathering darkness, a woman of this world wrapped in a shroud of ethereal mystery.

When Arthur arrived at the gatehouse, he found Bedwyr organising the teulu as they went about their task of tending the wounded and burying the dead.

'What of Illan and the Irish?' Arthur asked, his eyes scanning the coast for beacons or flames, for a hint that the Irish had landed.

'Illan saw the rout,' Bedwyr said, his arm outstretched, his forefinger pointing to a trail of lanterns as they drifted out to sea. 'The Irish did not commit to the battle and now they are returning to their homeland.'

Arthur nodded as though satisfied; the truce with the Irish would remain. True, war had dented the shield of mutual trust. However, the Pendragon and Illan would make amends over time; through trade, they would restore a sense of mutual respect and understanding.

As the Irish lanterns slowly faded into the distance, Cai approached with Marc and Gwenhwyfar at his side. Marc's hands were bound with strands of yew while his face was streaked in mud, sweat and blood.

'They were seeking to escape,' Cai explained, his sword levelled at Marc's abdomen.

Although it was a painful effort, Marc managed to twist his battle-scarred features into a smile. 'What are you waiting for?' he said, holding out his hands in submissive fashion before bowing his head towards Arthur. 'Claim your prize; take your revenge.'

With his face impassive and his eyes still, Arthur drew his sword. Holding Caledfwlch at arm's length, he took careful aim. Gwenhwyfar screamed, then, with one violent sweep of the blade, Arthur sliced through Marc's bonds, grazing his wrist in the process.

'I have no further need of revenge,' Arthur said, sheathing his sword. 'And my prize would be your loyalty, but your loyalty has been pledged to another.'

'I did not betray you,' Marc said in all sincerity. Holding his tongue, Arthur looked on askance. 'It is true,' Marc continued, 'I did offer my support to the Saxons, but for practical reasons, not reasons born out of love.'

'You thought that the Saxons would win the Battle of Badon,' Arthur said. 'You underestimated me and my people, but you will never underestimate us again.'

'You can leave Badon unharmed,' Arthur added. 'However, you are banished to Armorica. If you should return, I will seek you out and I will not be so merciful.'

'And what of me?' Gwenhwyfar cried, her hands covering her face, hiding her pitiful expression.

'You too are exiled,' Arthur said.

'But I love this land,' Gwenhwyfar pleaded.

'You love Marc,' Arthur said simply. Then, he nodded towards Cai, instructing his companion to escort Marc and Gwenhwyfar to the shore and away from Glywysing.

Arthur glanced down to the cuts and the grazes on his fingers, minor wounds that caused no pain. Conversely, as he gazed at Marc and Gwenhwyfar and watched them disappear into the darkness, he felt the ache of betrayal. Then, sobbing with joy, Eleri came rushing towards him and, as they embraced, the ache faded, banished by the balm of love.

Chapter Thirty

The aftermath of the battle - burying the dead, tending the wounded, gathering discarded weapons, seeking rewards - took the people of Badon through the darkness of night towards the light of a new day. As dawn was about to break, to reveal a cloudless sky, Arthur met Ambrosius and the tribal leaders at the burnt-out villa.

Wandering through the shell of the exedra, the villa's inner sanctum, Ambrosius stooped and gathered up a handful of charred tesserae. Staring at the once-colourful pieces of stone, he sighed: 'Is this the end of our relationship with Rome?'

'Rome has been dominant for many years,' Arthur replied. 'Many people know only the Christian message; that message will prove stronger than any building of stone.'

'So,' Ambrosius added wistfully, 'I have fought a righteous battle?'

'Without you, we would have no place to call home.'

Apparently satisfied, Ambrosius nodded. Then, he dropped the tesserae on to the ground and followed Arthur into the courtyard.

'Congratulations, Arthur!' Caradog grinned, his milk-white teeth gleaming against the backdrop of his smoke-stained face. 'The Saxons have lost their leaders; they will not be a threat for a generation or more.'

'What of Marc?' Vortipor asked quizzically. 'Has anyone seen Marc of Dumnonia?'

'Marc fled from the battle,' Cai said cheerfully. 'He fled from this island; Dumnonia is now under Arthur's control.'

'And good riddance to Marc!' Caradog added emphatically. Turning to face the tribal leaders, Caradog said: 'We gathered here to validate a new Pendragon. Before we leave, that task must be accomplished.'

'I nominated Arthur,' Ambrosius said, 'and I see no reason to change my mind. He is a man of principle and integrity. He has won twelve battles against the Saxons, more than any man gathered here today. He is the strongest candidate. He has fought for all the tribal leaders and he holds no favour or prejudice. More importantly, God has revealed that Arthur is the man to lead us; no other warlord would have won at Badon.'

'What say you, Caradog?' Bedwyr asked.

'Arthur has my sword.'

'What say you, Vortipor?'

'I bow before Arthur.'

'What say you, Cadwallon?'

'Our swords and our men helped you to secure victory.'

'True,' Arthur said with a wry smile. 'And I am sure that you are noble enough to recall that my sword saved your life.'

Pursing his lips in rueful fashion, Cadwallon nodded slowly. 'Arthur is our leader,' he acknowledged, 'Arthur is our Pendragon.'

'What say the people of Powys?' Bedwyr asked, his gaze fixed on Morganna.

'The people of Powys will support Arthur,' Morganna said, before offering a brief, mischievous smile.

'What say the people of Ergyng?'

'The people of Ergyng will embrace Arthur as one of their own,' Eleri said with pride.

With an indomitable look on his face, Ambrosius walked over to Arthur and placed ageing hands upon broad shoulders. 'Will you accept the honour of leading us as Pendragon?' Ambrosius asked.

'I will,' Arthur nodded. 'But on one condition: all gathered here must accept Eleri as my wife.'

'I accept your choice of wife,' Ambrosius said without hesitation. Turning to face the tribal leaders, he added: 'Should any man or woman claim opposition to this union, speak now or forever hold your peace.'

On a nearby farmstead a dog barked, the only sound to disturb the tribal leaders' silence.

'Very well,' Ambrosius said. With a look of quiet satisfaction gracing his face, the old warrior turned to his right and addressed the spiritual leader of the Britons: 'Archbishop Dyfrig: the Church will offer its blessing.'

'But Arthur wore a druidic token in battle,' Dyfrig complained, his swollen fingers wrapped around his wooden cross. 'Now he is taking a druidic wife; he is no longer pure of Rome.'

Glowering, then rumbling like thunder, Ambrosius replied: 'Step forward any man who can claim purity. None of us are saints. Look around you; our very existence depends on sin. Arthur is right; every man and woman should have the freedom to pray to the god of his or her choice. I will tell you all now, I will pray to the God of Rome. I will do so with the faith and the knowledge that I pray to the one true God and that that God will be open and tolerant to all men and women, regardless of their beliefs. After all, isn't that the ethos of God's message?'

Casting his eyes down to the ground, Archbishop Dyfrig offered the noble leaders a view of his balding pate. Releasing his wooden cross, he uttered a quiet prayer before lapsing into silence.

'Now bless Arthur as the new Pendragon,' Ambrosius instructed.

'The Church blesses you, Arthur, as our leader and Pendragon. Even so, no matter what your glory, your deeds will not be recorded in the Church annals.'

Stepping forward, Bedwyr said: 'If your words hold true, then you will do our people a great disservice. Furthermore, if Arthur's deeds are worthy of recognition, then the poets will record those deeds and the bards will sing his praises.'

Taking Eleri by the hand, Arthur climbed a nearby mound and gazed across the fields, the woodlands and the mountains. His eyes settled on the coast and the tranquil waters, free of vessels, be they hostile or friendly traders. The early morning sun offered a view of Dumnonia, distant, and yet soon to become familiar as Arthur claimed the right to rule over Marc's land.

Turning to the tribal leaders, Arthur said: 'I thank Ambrosius for his strength and his courage in leading us as Pendragon. Like him, I will continue to worship God but, at the same time, I will not turn my back on the ancestors. Under my leadership, men and women will be free to worship as they please, united in their love of this land, entwined by a common kindred and kin, bonded by time-honoured traditions.'

While the tribal leaders murmured in general agreement, Eleri stood on tiptoe and offered Arthur a kiss. Then, Arthur followed Eleri's gaze to the nearby mountain and a figure standing proud and alone, clutching a wooden staff adorned with a goat's skull.

'A druid?' Eleri asked, her eyes narrowing as she brought the man into focus.

'A Cymro,' Arthur replied, 'a fellow countryman. Later this day we will talk with him.'

Then, the sun rose over the forest man's shoulder and the land of Glywysing was bathed in warmth and light.

TANGWSTYL

by Mansel Jones

Tangwstyl is a story of love and murder, of loyalty and betrayal. Set in the medieval town of Kenfig in the year 1399, the story centres on a prophecy made by Merlin and the birth of a girl, named Tangwstyl. Based on historical fact, Tangwstyl tells the story of King Richard and a plot to assassinate him, of Owain Glyn Dwr and his struggle for personal and national justice, and of the medieval Church and its desire to suppress all forms of heresy. Tangwstyl also tells the story of the common men and women of Kenfig, ordinary people caught up in extraordinary events, events that would alter long held beliefs and reshape lives.

You can read more about Tangwstyl, including reviews, background details and extracts on http://tangwstyl.com

A HISTORY OF KENFIG

by Mansel Jones

A History of Kenfig tells the story of Kenfig and its neighbouring villages, Cefn Cribwr, Cornelly, Kenfig Hill, Pyle, Stormy Down and Sker from prehistoric times to the 20th century. In A History of Kenfig you can discover what really happened to Elizabeth Williams, the 'Maid of Sker', how a Roman road still dominates the village of Cornelly, whether the medieval town of Kenfig is under the pool or under the sand, how a famous sportsman helped to shape Cefn Cribwr's industrial landscape, the first person to legally build a house in Kenfig Hill and much more.

A History of Kenfig focuses on the people and events that have helped to shape the region and the breadth and range of the book are sure to appeal to the history lover and the general reader alike.

In 2012 Kenfig featured on the popular archaeology series Time Team and you can view that programme and read more about Kenfig on http://kenfigtimes.com

PENDRAGON

by Mansel Jones

You can read background details about Pendragon and articles about King Arthur on the Pendragon website http://pendragon497.com

ABOUT THE AUTHOR

Mansel Jones has been researching and writing about Arthurian, medieval and social history for the past twenty-five years. To date, Mansel has written three books: A History of Kenfig, Tangwstyl and Pendragon. A fourth book, a crime novel set in 1976, will follow in the near future.

You can read more about Mansel, his research and his articles on the websites http://www.mansel-jones.com and http://jonesthebook.com